Excerpt from Love's Christmas Gift

Elizabeth slipped around the back of the tree. She
wrapped her arms around the tree trunk and wiggled her
fingers. Bill chuckled. It looked like the tree had
moving arms. Bill placed a strand of lights in her hands.
His fingers touched hers, and for a minute, he felt a jolt.
Bill shook his head. He was just tired and hungry. He
hadn't eaten lunch and it was almost time for dinner.
Unplugged tree lights ⦀⦀⦀⦀⦀⦀⦀⦀⦀⦀⦀⦀⦀⦀⦀⦀
electricity.   ⟨ᗧ **S0-CFO-801**

Bill waited as Elizabeth carefully threaded the lights
through the branches on her side of the tree and passed
them back to him. Gradually, he worked them up into
the branches above him and passed them back to her.
Each time, his fingers touched hers, a small jolt shot
through his fingertips. Maybe he needed to see a doctor.
He hoped there wasn't something wrong with the
nerves in his fingertips.

When the lights were completely woven among the tree
branches, Elizabeth stepped from behind the tree. She
flicked on a switch at the front base of the tree. The tree
twinkled and sparkled.

"I never knew a tree could look so beautiful," Bill said,
looking at Elizabeth's glowing face in the tree light.

"It is magic, isn't it?" Elizabeth said softly. She looked
up at Bill. In her eyes, the magic spark of Christmas
twinkled.

May you have romance in all seasons!

Romance for all
the Seasons

Mindy Hardwick

Mindy Hardwick

ISBN-13:978-1495413278

ISBN-10:1495413276

DEDICATION

For those who find romance on the wide open seas and those who seek love in historic hotels. May every season be filled with old-fashioned romance.

Vintage Valentine

"Why is this the first time we've visited Grandma and Grandpa?" Ten-year-old Caitlin carefully cut out a red construction paper heart. She added it to the pile of pink and red hearts on the card table. "They always visit us."

"Grandma and Grandpa like to visit us," Hailey said. She swallowed hard and twirled the pearl ring she wore on her right ring finger. "It isn't easy for me to get time off from work." Hailey prayed her daughter couldn't tell she was lying. The truth was Hailey's boss begged her to take time off for years. It wasn't until the non-profit failed to receive an important grant, and Hailey lost her job, that she was able to think about time off.

"I like it here," Caitlin said. "It's interesting."

Hailey chuckled. The Elmheart Hotel her grandparents owned and operated was interesting. The hotel had been built in the late 1800's. It was the last standing hotel on the shores of Lake Ontario—a remnant from a bygone era.

As a child, Hailey loved listening to her grandmother talk about the glory days of the hotel. The Elmheart had been at the end of the Manitou trolley line. People took the trolley from Rochester to the beach to play baseball, swim, drink beer, and spend the night at the hotel. The hotel had large arches, stained glass windows, pine paneling on the walls of the seventeen bedrooms, and a hard maple floor in the dance hall. Grandfather inherited the hotel from his father. He married Grandma and the two settled down to raise their growing family along with their hotel business. As a child, Hailey could remember more than one Christmas unwrapping presents in the hotel's glorious living room under a large tree decorated with festive ornaments, ribbons, lights and tinsel. The Elmheart Hotel had been her grandparents' place of enchantment and celebrating their fiftieth wedding anniversary at the hotel would be perfect.

"Maybe we can live here!" Caitlin looked up. Her bright blue eyes locked with Hailey's. Hailey inhaled sharply. Caitlin had her father's eyes, and no matter how many times she looked at her daughter, Hailey never stopped feeling a small tightening in her stomach.

"I don't know," she said, and pressed her lips together. "I'm not sure where we will live." At least that was the truth. After her aunt died, Hailey tried to hang on to her aunt's home in Kansas City. But it'd become impossible and the house eventually fell into foreclosure. Things had gone from bad to worse since her aunt passed away. Caitlin's grades had slipped as she began having problems with some other girls in her class, and Hailey's job as office manager had unexpectedly terminated. When Hailey received the white and gold envelope announcing her Grandparents' fiftieth wedding anniversary, Hailey knew they should attend. Her grandparents were not getting any younger. It was time she went home to the small western, town in New York. It was time to face up to the lingering ghosts of her past.

Hailey looked up at the tall, arched ceiling and the pine paneling of the Elmheart Hotel's living room. The last time she'd been inside her grandparents' hotel was ten years ago. She was eighteen and three months pregnant. On a bright, August morning, Hailey stood in the large, sunlit, hallway. A small, denim duffel bag rested at her feet. She hugged her grandparents good-bye and walked out to a taxi which would take her to the train station. The train would take her to Kansas City where she would start a new life with her baby and aunt. Hailey's parents were devastated to find her pregnant. Hailey's dad declared all of his hopes and dreams were dashed, and refused to speak to her. Occasionally, she received a phone call from Mom, but if Dad walked into the room, Mom quickly hung up while promising to call again soon. Soon after Hailey moved to Kansas City, her parents took jobs working as research assistants in Singapore. She barely heard from them anymore.

Hailey picked up a red construction paper heart and absently turned it over. A vanilla candle burned on the living room table. Her stomach growled, reminding her she hadn't eaten since early that morning when they left Kansas City. Caitlin scarfed down both her breakfast and a sandwich at the airport, but Hailey had been too nervous to eat. She glanced at the grandfather clock in the living room. It was just after three o'clock—too early for dinner, but not too early for a snack and a cup of hot chocolate. Hailey peered around Caitlin and into the dining room. A large oak table set for eight sat in the center of the room. A matching sideboard leaned against the deep burgundy-papered wall. A silver tea set with a cream and sugar pitcher sat on the red tablecloth. Grandma always kept an assortment of teas, hot chocolates, hot water, and a plate of cookies for guests. But, today, the sideboard was empty. Hailey frowned. Had Grandma forgotten to set out the afternoon snacks?

In the dance hall, next door to the living room, Hailey could hear tables and chairs being moved.

Grandpa's deep voice carried through the wall as he instructed where to set up each table. Above Hailey's head, Grandma's footsteps tread lightly on the hardwood floors as she opened room doors, searching for something. From the time Hailey was ten until she was sixteen, she attended International Schools. But, she loved nothing more than returning to her grandparent's hotel for holidays. She'd been thrilled to move back to the small village of Eaglewood for her senior year of high school and everything went well until that fateful moment during the senior graduation party. After that night, everything changed. She'd gone from being her father's beautiful daughter, with her whole life ahead of her, to a shame and a disgrace.

Tears gathered in Hailey's throat and she brushed away the painful feelings. She turned away so Caitlin wouldn't look up and see her tears. Snow fell outside the large bay window of the living room. Thick heavy green drapes were tied back with gold-tasseled ties. The lawn was already covered by at least ten inches of snow. Piles of shoveled snow lined the driveway, and a new cover of snow covered the black asphalt. It'd been snowing all afternoon, but Hailey didn't worry about the weather canceling her grandparent's party: it snowed all winter in western New York. Everyone managed to make their way around without problems. In elementary school, Hailey could count on her right hand the times she had a full day off from school for a snow day. Hailey wiggled her toes inside the too large, red, fur-lined slippers. Grandmother always kept a box of items guests left behind. This afternoon, when Hailey and Caitlin arrived, Grandma dug the slippers out of the box and insisted Hailey wear them. Caitlin was thrilled to dig inside the box and hunt for a pair of thick socks as if it was a treasure hunt.

Turning her attention back to her daughter, Hailey leaned close and in a tone that sounded more like best friends conspiring said, "Do you know what we could use to make this moment absolutely perfect?"

"Tissue paper to decorate the Valentines?" Caitlin asked hopefully.

"Well," Hailey said. Her light laughter danced around the room. "Yes, we could use some tissue paper, but this box of construction paper, dollies and scissors was all I found in Grandma's office." Hailey reached over and touched her daughter's long, silky blonde hair. Caitlin's hair was so unlike her own and so like…Hailey stopped herself. She wasn't going to think about Caitlin's father. He was only a memory. He was a high school picture she kept tucked away in her nightstand. A picture she pulled out when it'd been an extremely long day and she wanted a listening ear. "I think we need some hot chocolate," Hailey said.

"With marshmallows?" Caitlin asked. Her face shone with an inner glow of childhood optimism.

"Yes," Hailey said. "I'm sure we can find a marshmallow or two in the kitchen." She once had the same hopeful spirit as her daughter, but ten years of hard work and making ends meet, while being a single parent, had worn away at the edges of that optimism. Hailey pushed back her chair. Her slippered foot touched a threadbare piece of carpet. Hailey stared down at the thinning carpet and frowned. Grandpa always kept the Elmheart Hotel in pristine condition. It had been listed on all the best travel sites for years. Grandpa proudly displayed each' best travel site 'sticker on the glass door in the entryway. Hailey stood with her hands braced on the card table and listened. Other than her grandpa's work in the dance hall, and her grandmother's steps above her head, she hadn't heard guests all afternoon. She assumed the hotel would be packed with her grandparents' friends attending the anniversary party. Hailey remembered Grandma and Grandpa always hosted holiday parties. Everything from large Fourth of July barbeques to New Year's Eve dance parties in the ballroom. The parties were some of the best attended in the area. Grandma often hired musicians from the local university who performed everything from harp solos to the sounds of the Big Band era. People talked about the parties for weeks afterward while waiting eagerly for the next invitation to arrive. If guests were arriving to check in, a few of them should have arrived by now. Hailey made a note to talk to her grandmother about the hotel. She hoped nothing was wrong.

Hailey leaned over and kissed Caitlin lightly on the head. Caitlin looked up at her mom. Her eyes widened in surprise. "What was that for?"

"Because I love you," Hailey said, and squeezed her daughter's shoulder.

"I love you too, Mom," Caitlin said. She placed a pink paper cut-out heart in the stack. "This is going to be the best Valentine's Day ever!"

Hailey turned away from the living room and stepped lightly toward the kitchen. She felt happier than she had in a long time. She was glad to see Caitlin so cheerful about Valentine's Day. Caitlin had been having problems with the other girls in her class teasing and bullying her. They met with her teacher, but the problems still hadn't stopped. Girls could be so cruel-sometimes. Hailey dreaded thinking about what Valentine's Day might be for daughter. Thankfully, she was here and Caitlin wouldn't have to suffer a Valentine's Day in a classroom full of kids who decided not to give her Valentine cards.

Hailey pushed open the swinging kitchen door and bumped into a very solid body standing on the other side. "I'm so sorry," Hailey said quickly. "I didn't realize anyone was in the kitchen." She stepped away from the door and looked up into the face of the one man she swore she'd never see again.

"Can I help you with something?" Patrick asked. He wiped his hands on the white apron tied around his waist. The apron covered black jeans and he wore a white sweatshirt with SUNY, Albany written across the front. His hair was still the same sandy brown Hailey remembered from high school. She knew exactly how that hair felt when she'd run her hands through it— smooth and fine-textured, and when Patrick picked her up for a date, his hair was never quite dry and curled around the edges of his shirt collar.

Hailey inhaled sharply. She'd spent years remembering him; years of seeing Patrick when Caitlin looked at her with the same bright blue eyes. Now, here he was, in front of her. But, did he even remember her?

They only dated for six months at the end of high school. It was ten years later. How would she tell him about Caitlin?

Flustered, Hailey quickly headed for the far left hand cabinet. "I'm just going to make some hot chocolate. I won't be here long." Hailey reached up and swung open the cabinet to find a stack of cups and glasses. "Oh! I guess things have changed a little bit."

"The food is in the pantry." Patrick opened a door covered with chalk paint, the same kind Hailey used on Caitlin's bedroom room wall when her daughter wanted to color on the walls at age five. On the other side of the pantry door, there were floor-to-ceiling shelves with canister and box sizes in every shape filled with tomatoes, sauces, and rice. "The hotel doesn't serve a breakfast anymore. It only caters special events. We moved the pantry to make more room for the larger food items needed for special events."

"I guess I won't be able to find a packet of hot chocolate in those large cans?" She kept her eyes focused just slightly to the left of Patrick so she didn't have to meet him in the eye. Hailey hoped her voice sounded light and not filled with the anxieties that plagued her stomach.

"There might be some in here." Patrick stepped half-way into the pantry. Hailey couldn't help noticing Patrick was as fit as he'd been as a high school baseball player. But, now he'd filled out and become a man. His broad shoulders filled his sweatshirt and she knew that underneath the jeans she'd find toned legs.

"Here it is!" Patrick pulled out a large canister labeled, 'hot chocolate.' He waved it in the air before he popped the lid and peered inside. "It looks as though there is plenty in here. How many cups do you need?"

"Two," Hailey said. "One for me and one for my daughter." Suddenly, she swallowed hard, the words threatening to burst from her.

Our daughter.

Ten years ago, Hailey believed she was doing the right thing by not telling Patrick. She didn't want to take away his opportunity to go to college on his baseball scholarship. If she told him about her pregnancy, Hailey knew Patrick would have given up everything. That was the last thing she wanted. But now his daughter was in the other room. He should know Caitlin. Caitlin should know him. But, how was she going to tell either one of them?

14

The heat rose to Hailey's face. She had to escape the kitchen. She needed time to think. Quickly, Hailey backed toward the doorway.

Her hands touched the doorknob, as Patrick said softly, "Please don't leave, Hailey."

***

Patrick stood, motionless. He stared into the eyes of the girl he once loved more than anything. The girl he hoped to marry. The girl he lost because of his stupidity in trying to follow a dream that dissolved before it even began.

"Mom!" A young girl, who looked to be about seven or eight, stepped into the kitchen. She wore light blue jeans, a hooded sweatshirt and bright blue socks. Long blonde hair cascaded down her back. She could have been Hailey twenty-years ago. The girl placed her hands on her small hips. "I'm hungry!"

Patrick stepped backward and winced. His right knee ached the way it always did when he stood too long.

"Are you okay?" Hailey's eyebrows drew together. A small wrinkle formed in the space between them. She reached her hand out to him, and then

15

snapped it back as if she'd been caught doing something she shouldn't.

"I'm fine." Patrick shifted his weight to his left leg. He'd learned to compensate for the pain a long time ago. But what he couldn't wrap his mind around was Hailey. Hailey had a daughter, and most likely she was married. Quickly, he glanced down at her hands. She wore a pearl ring on her right ring finger but nothing on her left. Patrick's heart lifted. Don't go there, he warned himself. It didn't matter that Hailey wasn't wearing a wedding ring. The ring could be in the jewelry shop getting cleaned. She might have lost it. She might just choose not to wear one. And even if Hailey wasn't married, that didn't mean she didn't have someone she cared deeply about and who cared about her.

"I've got a pot of soup cooking," Patrick said, turning away from Hailey and toward Caitlin. "My kitchen helper, Devon, is always hungry. He should be here soon. He comes in after school to help with large events like the party tonight. Would you like some soup?"

Caitlin wrinkled her nose. "I only like chicken noodle soup. What kind are you cooking?"

"Caitlin!" Hailey said sharply. "Remember your manners."

"Chicken noodle," Patrick said. He smiled at Caitlin. "It's Devon's favorite soup too." Caitlin reminded him of his sister when she was younger. After their mom died, it was up to him to make the meals for both him and his sister, Angie. His dad, when not running the bar, was too busy drinking his dinner. Patrick quickly learned how to heat up a can of soup. He also discovered how to scour the floor of the bar for their lunch money. Sometimes, the bar's line cook gave Patrick and Angie a plate of buffalo wings for an after-school snack. Both of them enjoyed sitting at the bar with their feet dangling from the stools. But, one day the liquor board inspector showed up unexpectedly. The inspector gave Dad a large fine for allowing two underage kids in the bar. After that, Patrick had to slip into the kitchen and grab a to-go box stuffed with buffalo wings and fries. Now, Angie lived in Portland, Oregon. Patrick missed her a lot and seeing Caitlin made him smile in a way he hadn't since Angie moved.

"Chicken noodle soup sounds good," Caitlin said. "Where is the hot chocolate?" She scanned the kitchen as if she were a health department inspector.

"Right here." Patrick picked up the large canister from the counter. "There is a faucet at the sink that pours hot water. All you need is a couple heaping spoonfuls and you're good to go."

"What about marshmallows?" Caitlin continued with her questions.

"Caitlin," Hailey said. "That's enough." She pressed her lips together and gave her head a disapproving shake. Hailey's strawberry-blonde hair swung across her thin, cotton sweater revealing a hole near the top left hand shoulder. Patrick frowned. Hailey never wore clothes with holes in them. She always had beautiful clothing, expensive, and well-tailored to fit her small frame.

"But Mom," Caitlin whined, "you promised marshmallows."

"I did not," Hailey said. "You asked and I told you I would look."

Patrick chuckled. It was good to hear Hailey bantering back and forth with Caitlin. Family was something he wanted, but it was a wish he didn't voice to many people. It was hard, after what happened with his baseball dream, to want and wish for anything again. He'd learned the hard way what happened to those wishes and dreams. They could go up in smoke in a minute. Gone forever, leaving you an empty playing field and a hard, long run down the bases.

"Mmmm...." Patrick said. "I'm not sure about marshmallows. Why don't you hop over to the pantry and poke around?"

"Are you the hotel's cook?" Caitlin asked.

"I'm the Chef for special events." Patrick straightened. He was proud of his job as the hotel's Chef. It hadn't been easy to land the job. If it wasn't for the help of Frank Sullivan, his long-time mentor, he doubted he even would have been considered. When he walked into the interview, Mrs. Matthews immediately remembered him as her granddaughter's high school boyfriend. She hired him on the spot. Mr. Matthews had been a little cool to him, but he figured it was just his lack of experience. Patrick worked hard to build up the special events and functions at the hotel. He'd been working at turning the hotel back into a profitable business—something it hadn't been for years. Secretly, he hoped to find out a little bit more about what had happened to Hailey. Now that he had a career, he had something to offer her— not like before when he lived with illusions of becoming a professional ball player.

Caitlin nodded thoughtfully. "Mom cooks at our house. I don't have a dad, but I always thought it'd be nice to have a dad who cooked, too." She turned away from Patrick and scooped a heaping spoonful of chocolate mix into a yellow mug.

Patrick's heart twisted and ached for Caitlin. He knew what it was like to not have a parent. He glanced over at Hailey and noted she had gone completely pale. Quickly, Patrick reached over and grabbed a chair from the round table in the corner of the kitchen. He took Hailey's arm and gently guided her to the chair. "Is everything okay?" He leaned down. She smelled like sunlit meadows in the summer, and for a minute, he felt dizzy and wanted to sit down, too.

Hailey stared at Patrick's hand, still resting on her forearm. She gazed up with those wide, hazel eyes that used to make him melt.

"I'm okay," she mumbled. "It must be the heat in the kitchen. I've been cold all afternoon, and I just got a little warm."

"When Devon arrives, I'll have him start a fire in the living room fireplace." Patrick checked the digital clock on the stove. "He should be here in a few minutes. Maybe Caitlin would like to help, too." Patrick felt himself craving alone time with Hailey. He wanted to brush his lips across hers. Feel the softness of her cheek, run his hands through her hair, and breathe in more of her.

"Oh no," Hailey said, and struggled to stand up. "Caitlin doesn't know how to start a fire. In our house, we flip a wall switch and the fireplace comes to life."

"Nothing wrong with her learning, "Patrick said. "Devon is a good teacher. They'll be careful." He smiled at Hailey. Hailey was a good mom. He'd seen her natural instinct to mother in high school. There were always a handful of younger brothers and sisters attending the high school baseball games. Usually, they clustered together, playing in a pile of dirt, or running and playing tag among the bleachers. But, baseball games could be long, and often someone fell down during a game of bleacher tag. Hailey was always the first one to comfort the child, soothe away tears and bring a smile back.

As Patrick stood beside Hailey in the kitchen, old memories came flooding back. He'd met Hailey in chemistry class during senior year. Hailey had been out of school for a week with strep throat. By the time she returned, she was behind in her work. He agreed to tutor her. Everyone was always tutoring him in English and he was glad to have the opportunity to tutor someone else in something he enjoyed—science. He never meant to fall in love with her. He didn't have time for a girlfriend. Every college in Western New York was scouting him for a full ride baseball scholarship. But, Hailey wasn't like most girls who made themselves readily available to him. Hailey was quiet and reserved.

Gradually, as they worked together in chemistry class, Hailey told him about her dad and how he expected her to major in science and become a great researcher like himself. She told him how her mom was scared of her dad and his violent temper. Patrick wanted nothing more than to protect and shelter Hailey for the rest of her life. But first, he had to go to college on the baseball scholarship, and that was where he'd made the biggest mistake of his life—a mistake he wouldn't repeat. Patrick lightly trailed his hand along the back of Hailey's shoulders. He felt them stiffen, and then relax slightly as he gently applied pressure in a soft massage. Whatever Hailey's life had become, she carried a lot of stress in her shoulders, and that was one thing he wanted to take away for her.

***

Hailey closed her eyes. She melted into Patrick's firm hands as he massaged her shoulders. It'd been so long since she'd felt the touch of a man. So long since

22

she'd let herself relax. A small moan threatened to escape Hailey's lips.

Suddenly, the sound of a crash caused Hailey to open her eyes and jerk away from Patrick. A teenage boy, wearing a large green parka, stood in the kitchen door leading to the backyard porch. A blast of cold air and snow spiraled into the room from the open door. A small white cord dangled down the front of the boy's jacket. He moved along in a rhythmic dance to the music which pumped into his ears from the earplugs. It was turned up so loud, Hailey could hear the beat. A woman wearing a deep maroon, wool coat, and a colorful scarf tied around her long dark hair, stepped up behind Devon. She firmly shut the door. In her arms, she carried a large basket.

"Devon!" Patrick said. "Cassie!"

Cassie set the basket on the island countertop. "Sorry, we're a little late. The lake roads haven't been plowed. If it gets too much worse, we'll have to walk home!"

"Hailey!" Cassie quickly crossed the black and white kitchen tile floor. She embraced Hailey in a warm hug. "It's so good to see you again!"

"You too!" Hailey met Cassie while working on a high school senior project. Cassie was a couple years older than Hailey and attending the local community college. She taught after-school art classes to the elementary school kids. Hailey's project was to create an art and science fair with the elementary school kids. She wanted to show how the two could blend together. They spent many hours working together and it was good to see her again.

"What's in the basket?" Caitlin asked as she bounced over to the counter.

"Who is this?" Cassie asked as she unwrapped her scarf.

"This is my daughter," Hailey said slowly. "Caitlin, this is Cassie." Hailey crossed her fingers behind her back. She hoped Cassie would not see the connection between Patrick and Caitlin.

"Very nice to meet you," Cassie said. "Devon is my husband's nephew. He lives with us." She stepped over to Devon who leaned against the kitchen wall. Cassie yanked the earplugs out of Devon's ears.

"Sorry." Devon mumbled. He unzipped his jacket and stuck his earphones inside the coat pocket.

Hailey smiled. The kitchen bubbled with life. It was what she remembered about The Elmheart Hotel. There were always neighbors stopping by, friends and family playing games, and long evenings talking and reading by the fireplace. It was good to be back.

A silver, candy heart form stuck out of the basket. "Where did you get this?" Hailey exclaimed. She scooped the heart out of the basket and turned it over in her hands.

"I found it at an estate sale a couple years ago," Cassie said. "There are a couple more in the basket. I haven't had a chance to use them yet. But I thought they'd be great for making party favors." Cassie reached into a red and white, hand-woven bag she carried over her left shoulder. She pulled out a stack of small, red fabric bags. Each bag was decorated individually with swirling hearts.

Caitlin scooted closer to Cassie, and pressed against her side. "Those are really great! Did you make them?"

"Yes," Cassie handed a bag to Caitlin. "The Matthews have donated quite a bit of time and money over the years to the Teen Art Center. I wanted to contribute to their party."

A lump formed in Hailey's throat. She had lived with her aunt for the last ten years. They lived in a suburb of Kansas City. There was no past or shared history with her family. Her aunt always said she liked it that way. She said it was too claustrophobic to live in the small town where she'd grown up and everyone knew her life story. Hailey believed living in a town where she had no history was ideal for having a baby she didn't want anyone to know about. But, now, Hailey bit her lower lip. Had she been mistaken?

"Mom?" Caitlin touched Hailey's arm.

Hailey looked up, but she didn't look at Caitlin. Instead, she stared across Caitlin's head and into Patrick's warm, blue eyes.

Hailey shifted her attention to her daughter. She cleared her throat. "Yes?"

"Do you think Cassie could help with the Valentines? She's an artist!"

"I'd love to help with the decorations!" Cassie squeezed Caitlin's shoulder. "Show me what to do!"

"Devon," Patrick said smoothly, "can you start a fire in the living room? A fire should have been started hours ago."

"Sure thing, boss." Devon ambled toward the door. He paused and held it open as Cassie and Caitlin scrambled through, both talking quickly about colors, textures, and all the ideas they had for decorating.

"Well." Hailey turned back to the basket. She pulled out two more heart candy molds and a bag of chocolate. "I guess we better get to work." Suddenly, the silence in the kitchen was deafening.

"I'm pretty sure we have better chocolate in the pantry than what's in those bags. I'll just store that chocolate for another occasion." In two long strides, Patrick stepped up beside Hailey. His musky aftershave smelled like a deep forest as his side touched hers. He leaned over, but instead of picking up the chocolate bags, his fingers gently caressed hers. "I missed you, Hailey," Patrick said softly.

Hailey's insides shivered. She shyly gazed up at him. She missed him too. She'd wished for him so often when Caitlin hit her first milestones: the first time she learned to talk, the first time she learned to walk, and her first day of school. But, Hailey never could have told Patrick about Caitlin. He had a full scholarship. A baseball career was waiting for him. He would have given up everything for her and Caitlin and she didn't want him to do that. He would have ended up working in his father's bar and never fulfilling any of his dreams.

"How is baseball?" Hailey asked brightly. "I don't really keep up with too many sports."

A dark shadow crossed Patrick's face. He removed his hand from Hailey's and looked at the ground. When he lifted his head, his eyes were veiled in a dark coldness that made her suck in her breath.

"I don't play baseball," Patrick said. "I blew out my knee during freshman practice. I lost my scholarship. I never played a game."

"Oh, Patrick." Hailey immediately stepped forward. She placed her hand on Patrick's arm. Her heart ached for him and she wanted desperately to comfort him and take away all the pain. His dream. His wonderful baseball dream had never materialized.

"I had some rough years," Patrick said. His voice was flat. "I worked at my dad's bar for awhile. I was pretty depressed and started drinking a lot. One night, Frank Sullivan came in. He always liked my high school games. He heard what happened and took me under his wing as a line cook in his restaurant. A couple years later, I went back to school and got my degree in culinary arts. It's worked out. I like cooking."

Hailey's emotions crashed inside her. Life could be so cruel, sometimes. Patrick lost his scholarship. He never went to college to become a ball player. Hailey wanted to sit down on the floor and sob. All the years she believed he was happily working away at his dream. And even worse, she'd prided herself on never asking about Patrick. She thought it was best not to know anything. But she was wrong. She should have asked her grandparents about him. They would have told her what happened. She should have told Patrick about Caitlin years ago. He'd missed ten years of Caitlin's life because of her. Suddenly, the world felt like it was closing in on her. Her legs wobbled underneath her.

Patrick stepped forward and pulled her into his arms before she hit the floor. She melted against his hard, solid chest. His arms wrapped around her and she gazed up at him.

"Patrick," she said.

"Shhh…" he lowered his lips to hers. Softly at first, he pressed his warm lips against hers. She wanted to turn away; stop him from kissing her. She wanted to stop herself from falling over the edge and in love with him again, but she couldn't. She parted her lips and opened to him. Moaning softly, she surrendered to the kiss. She shifted and moved so she could wrap her arms around Patrick. Her fingers brushed past Caitlin's hot chocolate mug on the counter behind them.

Suddenly, Hailey broke away from Patrick. She could not fall in love with Patrick; not without telling him about Caitlin. But, now was not the right time. There was too much going on. After the party tonight, she'd tell him. She would take him aside and tell him everything. Hailey licked her lips and smoothed her hands over her sweater. She turned away from Patrick

***

Patrick stared at Hailey's back. He clenched his jaw. He'd been a fool to kiss her. He felt an irresistible pull to Hailey. He was swept away in the moment—just like the night of their senior graduation party. That night, they snuck away to a small boathouse at the back of a classmate's large lakeside home. Patrick planned to do nothing but talk and kiss. Hailey wasn't the type of girl to lose her virginity in a boathouse at a senior graduation party. But, maybe it was because everything was changing. Maybe it was the feeling of being invincible as graduating seniors. Whatever it was, they both allowed the moment to overtake them.

When he dropped Hailey off at her house, she kissed him softly and he promised to see her after he got back from summer ball camp at the college. But by the time he got back in August, Hailey was gone. He heard she went to live with an aunt, somewhere in the Midwest. He tried to call but her cell phone was discontinued. He tried to find her parents, but they had moved overseas. He didn't want to bother her grandparents with what everyone kept telling him was only a high school fling. In September, he headed off to college and tried to put thoughts of Hailey behind him. But he couldn't. He spent the entire first semester thinking about her, dreaming about her, and not wanting to date anyone else. That spring, he hoped to escape back into baseball. But, he blew out his knee and all interest in Hailey, or anything else, left him. In one moment, Patrick became a failure. He had nothing to offer anyone.

Now, ten-years later, he did have something to offer. But, again she was pulling away. Patrick steeled himself. He needed to get away from the kitchen. He needed to get his emotions under control. Patrick strode to the swinging kitchen door and pushed it open. He gave the door a harder push than necessary, and the door slammed against the wall. In the living room, a warm fire crackled in the fireplace. Devon was nowhere to be seen, but Caitlin and Cassie sat on folding chairs at a cardboard table. A pile of cut-out red hearts and a box of what looked like old- fashioned valentine cards lay in front of them.

"Look what Grandma found!" Caitlin popped up from her chair. She ran over to Patrick and waved a small pink and red valentine card. Patrick smiled down at the young girl. He wished Hailey shared more of her daughter's enthusiasm about him.

"Take my seat," Cassie said as she stood. She stretched her arms to the ceiling and did a quick side bend. "I'll go check on Eric and Devon in the ballroom. Surely, the tables and chairs must be set up." Cassie swirled around in the direction of the ballroom.

Patrick gingerly sat down at the table with Caitlin. "I don't know if I can help you too much," he said. "I'm afraid all my creative talents lie in the kitchen." Hesitantly, he picked up one of the valentines. The edges were faded yellow. A plump, round boy handed a valentine to a young girl who wore a blue gingham dress and stood bashfully by his side. "Be Mine." the card read. Patrick sighed. If only it could be that easy.

"Did you and my mom have a fight?" Caitlin asked.

Patrick smiled and shook his head. "Not really."

"We fight sometimes." Carefully, Caitlin ran a stick of glue over the backside of a valentine. "It doesn't last for very long."

"That's good to know." Patrick fiddled with a stack of construction paper red hearts. A valentine was pasted on each one. A single piece of red string looped through a small hole punched at the top of the heart. "You're pretty good with these decorations."

"Last year for my birthday," Caitlin said, "I made all the decorations!" She glued the valentine to a large red, heart.

"That's great!" Patrick eyed Caitlin. "How old are you? Eight?"

"Ten!" Caitlin said proudly.

"Ten." Patrick dropped the valentine. He looked hard at Caitlin. Caitlin was ten. Ten years ago, he spent the night with Hailey in the boathouse. Patrick swallowed. It wasn't a coincidence that Caitlin looked like his sister. Patrick didn't know whether to cry, or get up and shout from the top of the hotel's balcony that he had a daughter. He had a daughter!

Suddenly, his insides deflated. But, why had Hailey kept it from him all these years? Why hadn't she told him?

****

Hailey dipped a soup ladle into the thick, melted chocolate. Carefully, she poured the chocolate into a silver heart-shaped form. Her mouth watered as she ran her finger alongside the ladle.

"What is that delicious smell?" Ellen Matthews pushed open the kitchen door and stepped inside. Short grey hair framed her heart-shaped face and her brown eyes danced. Ellen wore a simple black skirt with a red top. A pink and red scarf draped around her neck and heart-shaped gold earrings dangled from her ears.

.

"What is that delicious smell?" Ellen Matthews pushed open the kitchen door and stepped inside. Short grey hair framed her heart-shaped face and her brown eyes danced. Ellen wore a simple black skirt with a red top. A pink and red scarf draped around her neck and heart-shaped gold earrings dangled from her ears. "Chocolate hearts, Grandma" Hailey said. "The molds aren't quite ready yet, but you could help me lick the pan." Hailey lifted the heavy saucepan from the stovetop.

"I'll just wait until tonight," Ellen said. "Thank you, dear. Everyone is doing such a wonderful job helping out with this party."

Hailey set the pan in the sink and ran the water. When the pan filled, she turned the water off, and reached around to untie her apron. Hanging the apron back on a small hook by the door, Hailey looked up at her grandma. Her blue eyes looked more tired than Hailey remembered.

"Is everything okay?" Hailey asked. "Grandpa? He's...."

"He's fine, dear." Ellen waved her hand airily. "I sent him upstairs to take a quick nap before the guests arrive."

Ellen pulled out a wood chair tucked underneath a small, round table in a corner of the kitchen. The table was covered by a sunflower tablecloth and matching cushions were tied to the chair. "But, I do want to talk to you about something."

Hailey quickly sat down. Her heart raced. Was something the matter with Grandma?

"I've always loved this spot," Ellen said. She stared wistfully toward the door leading outside. "I love watching the birds at the feeder. In the Spring, you can see the crocuses and it's the perfect view for summer fireworks."

"The Elmheart is a very special place," Hailey said. "I have always loved it." She leaned over and softly squeezed Grandma's hand.

"We've decided to put the hotel up for sale," Ellen said. Her voice cracked and her face etched with sorrow.

"For sale!" Hailey's heart dove into her slippers.

"It wasn't an easy decision, but we aren't getting any younger, and guests just don't fill the hotel the way they used to."

"But what about the special events?" Hailey's voice arched an octave.

"Those help," Ellen said, "but people aren't staying here anymore. It used to be we threw a party and the hotel would book months in advance. But now, everyone just wants the hotels with pools and free internet."

"Free internet is easy to solve," Hailey said. "All you need is…"

"Ah, dear," Ellen said. "Grandfather and I don't want to turn this hotel into a chain hotel with free internet, pools and spas. When we bought the hotel, we envisioned it as a timeless, classic place. It's a place where people can leave their worries of the real world behind. It's a place where we don't need a computer in every room. It's a place where people connect with each other."

"Specials!" Hailey leaned forward in her chair. She tapped the tabletop with her fingers. "Have you run a special lately? Two nights for the price of one?"

Ellen shook her head. Her heart earrings bobbed. "Sometimes, you just have to know when to let go. I think this might be one of those cases. It just might be time to let go of the hotel."

Hailey felt tears bubbling in her throat. Her grandparents had always owned the Elmheart Hotel. If they sold it, someone would probably tear it down and build condos on the waterfront. Someone who didn't understand the history. Someone who didn't understand the long-standing traditions of the hotel.

"Your grandfather and I want our engagement party to be the last event we host; a final way to say good-bye." Ellen squeezed Hailey's hand. "We're so glad you and Caitlin could come."

A tear rolled down Hailey's face. "I'm glad we could be here too, Grandma. You and Grandpa mean a lot to me." Hailey reached up and wiped away her tears. Ellen slipped her hand into her skirt pocket. She pulled out a red, cloth handkerchief and handed it to Hailey.

Hailey blew her nose as Ellen said, "Shall we go see how the decorating is going?"

"Of course." Hailey slipped the handkerchief into her pocket. She stood and linking her arm with her grandmother's, walked out of the kitchen and into the living room. Her mind raced. There had to be a way to save the Elmheart Hotel.

In the living room, Devon, Cassie and Eric sat on the floor at the coffee table. In front of them was a large stack of red, cut-out hearts and vintage valentines. Patrick perched on a tall ladder, hanging each cut-out vintage valentine by a thick piece of red ribbon. Caitlin stood below him, directing and holding the ladder.

"What a perfect idea!" Ellen exclaimed. She walked slowly up to one of the vintage valentines. "We've had these valentines in the closet for years. They were valentines Grandfather and I exchanged when we were in elementary school. I'm so glad we've been able to give them new life."

Patrick shifted and the ladder wobbled. Hailey gasped. Quickly, she stepped around Caitlin and placed her hands on the ladder.

"Thanks," Patrick said, his warm blue eyes meeting hers. "I think I might have almost lost it."

"Do you have any more valentine cards?" Caitlin held up an empty box. "We could scatter the valentine cards on the table. Everyone could take one home."

"What a wonderful idea!" Ellen dropped her arm around Caitlin, and pulled her close. "I believe we have another box upstairs, if not two or three. Why don't you come with me and we'll see what we can find?"

Eric stood up and stretched. He glanced at the clock. "I think we'll head on home and get dressed for the evening."

Suddenly, Caitlin broke free from under Ellen's arm. She dashed over to Devon. "I have something for you," she said shyly. Reaching into her pocket, Caitlin pulled out one of the vintage valentines. "I saved this one just for you."

Devon's ears turned pink as he took the card from Caitlin. "Thanks," he said gruffly.

Caitlin danced away from Devon and back to the stairs. "Come on, Grandma!" She called. "Let's go find those Valentines."

Cassie, Eric, and Devon pulled on coats, mittens, and scarves, and saying their good-byes, headed out of the door.

Caitlin is a great kid." Patrick climbed down from the ladder and stood beside Hailey. His shoulders brushed hers.

"Yes," Hailey replied, "she is a great kid."

"She's our daughter." Patrick said quietly.

Hailey inhaled sharply. Her stomach churned. "How did you..."

"I didn't know at first. I'm not very good at guessing a kid's age. I thought she was about eight-years old. But then, she mentioned her birthday. She's ten." Patrick turned and stared hard at Hailey.

"Yes," Hailey said, without removing her gaze from Patrick. "She is ten."

"Why didn't you tell me?" Patrick asked. "I would have been there. I would have taken care of you and her. I would have given up everything to be with you." His voice cracked.

"That's exactly why I didn't tell you," Hailey said as the tears pooled in her eyes. "I didn't want you to give up everything. I wanted you to have your dream. I wanted you to go to college. I wanted you to have your baseball career and make something of your life."

"I looked for you," Patrick said. "When I got back from baseball camp, I tried to find you. But everyone told me you were gone. They said it was just a high school fling, and I should forget about you. I couldn't forget you, Hailey. I couldn't. But, then, after I blew out my knee, I didn't think I had anything to offer. I was wrong."

Tears streamed down Hailey's face. "We were both wrong. We were both so wrong."

Patrick stepped closer to Hailey. He dropped his arm around her and pulled her close to him. "It's time to let this go," he said softly. "We can't undo what's been done. We can only move forward from this day and try to do things differently. If you and Caitlin are going to be in Kansas City, then I will move to Kansas City. I will be wherever you are. I will help you with whatever you need."

"We're not going back to Kansas City," Hailey said, slowly. "I lost my job and Caitlin is having problems with some girls in her class. Grandma said the hotel is up for sale. I was thinking if Caitlin and I moved here, I could try running the hotel. Grandma doesn't want to put in a pool or the internet, but there are other things we could do."

Patrick picked up a valentine from the table. He held it in the air. "Vintage."

"Vintage?"

"Old, charming, eclectic," Patrick said. "I think we could sell the hotel rooms on those words. I could make up a menu. We could serve breakfast and afternoon snacks in the living room."

"Oh, Patrick!" Hailey said. "Do you really think it would work?"

"I do," Patrick said. "Caitlin is pretty good with the decorations!"

"Yes," Hailey smiled. "She is."

Patrick leaned over and whispered against Hailey's cheek, "When do we tell Caitlin?"

"Today," Hailey said. "We tell Caitlin today."

"Happy Valentine's Day." Patrick lowered his lips to Hailey's.

"Happy Valentine's Day."

Love's Storm

Sabrina rummaged inside the mahogany desk drawer for a key to the Osprey Room. "It's here somewhere," she mumbled to herself. The Osprey Room was the smallest of the Bed and Breakfast's six rooms. But, Sabrina knew for the sailors racing in the Regatta there wouldn't be very much time spent in the room.

Sabrina took another look at the guest list. According to the register, all the men from Skipper Bill's roster had checked in, except for one. And he was registered for the Osprey Room. Sabrina yanked the drawer out, and tried to imagine the key materializing out of thin air. Of course, nothing happened.

"Is there a problem?"

"No." Sabrina said firmly as she shoved the drawer shut and looked up into smoky, jet black eyes.

Sabrina inhaled sharply. She'd know those eyes anywhere. She'd never forgot those jet, black eyes and the way they could make her stomach turn over and her heart pound. They were the eyes of her romantic teenage dreams. The eyes of the boy she had once been in love with. The boy who had broken her heart and she had sworn to forget. And, still, the eyes and his memories taunted her in her dreams.

Damon.

Even after ten years, her heart still dropped into the pit of her stomach.

"Saddie," Damon said in that same deep voice she remembered so well. The same deep voice which had been the last thing she'd heard before she went to sleep after hours of talking on the phone. Sometimes, as Sabrina watched her niece text to her boyfriend, she would ask, "But don't you miss hearing his voice?" Caitlin always said, "Oh, Aunt Sabrina, you are so old-fashioned! Everyone texts!" Now, hearing Damon's voice again, Sabrina was glad she was "old-fashioned."

Damon leaned forward and pressed his thigh against the desk. Sabrina smelled his spicy aftershave—different than the one he'd worn as a teen but underneath still the same deep earth smell which was Damon. As Sabrina swept her eyes over him, she couldn't help but notice that the past ten years had been good to him. At eighteen, Damon had always been fit from summers sailing in crew. But he'd still been a boy when she'd known him. Sabrina sucked in her breath. She knew her cheeks were flushed with the heat that was quickly rising through her. Now, he was a man.

And, no longer was she a girl of eighteen, unsure and unfamiliar with what could happen between a man and a woman. Now, every part of her was reminding her how it felt to be around a man who ignited a spark in her.

Gently, Damon picked up her left hand. He traced his finger over her empty ring finger.

"Not married."

Sabrina yanked her hand back and struggled to regain her senses. It didn't matter that she felt a little heady, and that the nearness of Damon was making her lose her senses. She had to pull it together. She was not going to risk falling for Damon, again. "No. Not married." Sabrina said curtly. Damon didn't need to know that her marriage to Andrew had lasted all of eighteen months before he'd been killed in a powerful, late fall storm. It had been one of the last races of the season, and they'd already had their first snowfall a few days before. During the race, the jib had crossed the bow of the boat, and knocked Andrew into the water. He'd hit his head, and immediately sank to the depths below.

Sabrina was left with a too large house and an aching heart. Over the last two years, she'd been able to turn the house into a successful Bed and Breakfast. The

Osprey B & B was known for both its warmth and hospitality. It didn't hurt that the house was in a prime location on the edge of Lake Ontario. Quietly, Sabrina tucked her broken heart away behind the business of running a successful Bed and Breakfast.

"The right guy hasn't come along." Damon smiled at her. He pushed back a lock of his jet black, curly hair, and Sabrina willed herself not to reach over and run her hands through his thick hair. She noticed that, he too, did not wear a wedding ring. It surprised her to see that Damon wasn't married. There had always been a flock of girls waiting in the wings for Damon, each girl hoping that he would choose her. Although, Sabrina glowered darkly, maybe Damon liked it that way. Maybe he was one of those men who had a different girl in every Port. He was probably looking to add her to the list. Well, she fumed. She wouldn't be on his list.

"If you'll excuse me a minute," Sabrina said curtly, as she reached for her cell phone. "I need to make a call. There seems to be a missing key."

"Take your time," Damon smiled at her and set down his blue denim duffle bag. "I'll just take a look around."

Sabrina strode quickly into the red and blue tiled mosaic courtyard. The cool air felt good on her hot cheeks.

Breathe, she told herself. Just breathe. The most important thing was finding the missing key. Sabrina brought her best friend, Cassie's name to the top of her cell contacts list. Cassie had helped clean the rooms this morning. It was possible, in the flurry of getting everything ready for the extra guests, that she had stuck the key in her pocket.

"Sabrina?" Cassie answered.

In the background, Sabrina could hear Cassie working at the Regatta's registration table, and from the male laughter around her, having a very good time. Cassie always had a good time, no matter what she did. She had an infectious smile and a quick laugh. Sabrina had been best friends with Cassie since high school. Senior year, Cassie had dated Damon's best friend, Eric. The four of them often hung out together after sailing races on the pier. If anyone understood how Sabrina felt about Damon, it was Cassie.

"Damon's here." Sabrina sank down into one of the small, black iron chairs at a black iron table she'd found at a flea market in Syracuse. She absently plucked a couple of rose petals from the small arrangement on the table.

"Oh Sabrina," Cassie said. "Do you want me to find a place for him?"

"No," Sabrina crossed her long shapely legs and looked out over the colorful courtyard. She enjoyed working in the garden, and this time of year, when everything was in full bloom, her hard work paid off. "I have a room. I just don't have a key." She'd been meaning to get an extra set of keys made for each room, but it seemed as though she never had time. The Bed and Breakfast ran on a tight budget, and unless they were hosting a wedding or other special event, Sabrina tried to make do with the minimum number of staff. Most of the time, "making-do" meant her, and a college girl who came over in the morning and straightened up the rooms after check-out.

Sabrina knew she should have had the keys made before the Regatta. Since the event had been announced, the whole town was turned upside down. Every hotel and inn had been filled for months. The Chamber of Commerce was thrilled when the town was selected to host the Regatta, and people talked about it for months. Sabrina even helped Cassie clean out her art studio and haul in a futon that would act as an extra bed for the sailors. Cassie's eyes had gleamed with excitement. All these men, she gushed. There has to be one for us. Sabrina only shook her head and smiled sadly at her best friend. The Regatta would be great business for her Bed and Breakfast and the town, but she wasn't looking for any more romantic attachments. Not with another sailor, and certainly not with Damon!

"Don't worry," Cassie said. "I'm sure I dumped the key into my bag."

"Thanks," Sabrina said. "I hope you can find it."

"Find what?" Damon pulled out the chair opposite Sabrina and lazily folded himself into it. He stretched his long legs out in front of him. Sabrina marveled at his muscle tone and deep tan.

"There's a small problem," Sabrina said to Damon. Her voice shook a small bit. She hoped he wouldn't notice. She'd always believed honesty was the best policy with her guests, a trait that served her well over the years when the Bed and Breakfast got double-booked or small incidents arose with a guest who was unhappy over something. Sabrina always tried her best to be honest. Now, trying to hold back the raging emotions inside of her when Damon's eyes met hers, she tried to treat Damon like everyone else—a guest at her Bed and Breakfast instead of the man she had once loved.

Sabrina cleared her throat. "We are missing your room key. Unfortunately, I only have one. I have not had time to get a master set made. Until we find the key, we will have to find a different place for you to sleep."

"I see," Damon leaned back in his chair and studied Sabrina. "And where do you sleep, Saddie?"

Sabrina shivered at the mention of the name she'd left behind in childhood. Only Damon could still make it sound sexy and enticing.

"The shed." Sabrina waved toward the small potting shed on the corner of the Inn's wide sweeping yard.

Damon looked horrified. "Surely, there must be room for you inside the Inn."

Sabrina's heart softened. Damon had always been protective of her. He always looked out for her best interest. It touched her he would still find a way to make sure she had a place to sleep. "It's okay," Sabrina said lightly. "There's a small futon in the shed. When I open the door, it's quite beautiful. I enjoy listening to the birds sing in the early morning hours, and the soft quiet of the night."

Damon dark eyes studied her for a minute before he reached out and gently picked up her hand. He caressed the insides of her palms before linking their fingers together.

Sabrina shivered with his touch, but she did not pull away. As he softly twined his fingers with hers, her stomach fluttered, and she knew that in an instant she could fall back in love with him.

"You always had a kind heart, Saddie." Damon said gently.

Feeling herself weaken towards him, Sabrina yanked her hand away. She wouldn't go there. She would not allow herself to get lost again in foolish romantic dreams. Not with Damon. She could not trust herself not to get hurt again.

"We are long past being over each other." Sabrina pushed herself away from Damon and stood. Her legs felt wobbly beneath her, and she grabbed onto the table to steady herself. How could he still make her feel this way after ten years?

"We are?" Damon questioned. His eyes searched hers.

Sabrina waivered. She wanted nothing more than to lean down and feel his soft lips on hers. She wanted to feel his arms wrap around her in that strong, protective embrace that always made her feel nothing could hurt her. Of course, she reminded herself, the thing that had hurt her had been him.

"Yes," Sabrina said firmly. This time her voice did not waiver.

"Why?" Damon said as he stood and moved next to her. His arm brushed her side, and she could feel his warm breath. His voice was husky and deep. "I wanted to see you again, Saddie."

Sabrina held very still. Had Damon returned because of her? His skipper had booked their rooms. Did Damon suggest her Bed and Breakfast to Bill? But, how could she trust him? How did she know he had changed?

Sabrina remembered, all too well, the last day she had seen Damon. She had been so excited. It was the end of the summer, and she wanted to surprise him. Sabrina had decided that this would be the night. The night when all the aching and longing for each other would finally result in a glorious coming together. It was something Damon had pushed for all summer, and Sabrina kept insisting the time wasn't right. But now, her parent's summer cabin was empty, and it was the last summer party before everyone went off to college. Sabrina knew now was the time. She had to find out how much Damon loved her and show him much she loved him. In a week, they would be separated by their colleges. She had chosen to stay in Rochester and attend one of the small liberal arts schools. And Damon was headed to Albany University. They'd be close enough to be together for long weekends and vacations, but they wouldn't see each other every day. They wouldn't be a part of each other's daily lives, and things would be different. Sabrina wanted Damon to know how much she loved him, and this seemed like the perfect time to do what both of them had been creeping closer and closer to all summer.

Earlier in the day, she and Cassie drove out to the small cottage and prepared it for what was supposed to be the best night of her life. But instead, everything had gone wrong. Horribly wrong. From the minute Damon had picked her up, he'd been cold and distant. Barely exchanging more than a hello, he had driven them to Cassie's end-of-the-summer party and spent most of the evening playing volleyball on the beach, while she wondered what on earth she had done to make their summer romance cool off so fast. The worst part was he'd ignored her not- so-subtle hints about her parents' summer cabin being empty, and instead driven her straight home. In her driveway, he'd told her that he felt it was best they go their separate ways. He had things to do, to accomplish, and a romance was only going to weigh him down. Shocked at his coldness, she had mutely pushed out of the car, tears rolling down her face before she hit the door. After a sleepless night, she barely remembered that she needed to go out to the cabin and collect the candles and lacy black lingerie she had left lying on the bed—all with the hopes that something wonderful might happen that summer evening.

Now, in the garden, Sabrina turned to face Damon. "We're grown-up, Damon," She stated. "Not eighteen." And, with a quick turn, she whisked away.

****

Damon watched Sabrina go. He knew she had every right to be cold to him. He'd been a first-class jerk at eighteen. He thought he needed to conquer the world rather than accept what the world was giving to him. Every night at college, he'd missed Sabrina. He'd wanted to call her, tell her he was wrong. But every time he reached for the phone, his heart stopped and he'd set the phone aside. She'd come too close to him, and it scared him. What if he couldn't please her? What if he couldn't give her what she wanted? He was barely eighteen. He hadn't explored the world. He didn't know who he was. How could he provide anything for her? So instead of spending his time with Saddie, he'd spent the last ten years building a successful career in the banking industry and sailing on the weekends. Although there had been women wanting to keep him warm at night, women who eagerly joined him for elaborate weekend jaunts to the Caribbean and Europe, none of the women had touched his heart like Saddie. She was the one he had never forgotten, and he'd come back to tell her.

Damon looked around the Bed and Breakfast courtyard. Saddie had done a nice job. What could have been a cold, large, and uninspiring falling-down house had turned into a beautiful and elegant welcoming Bed and Breakfast. Purple and white lilac bushes framed the well-kept yard, and small sitting areas with lavender and daisies had been tucked into small pocket corners by the fence. A white gate was left open and Damon could see the blue shores of Lake Ontario. Small white sailboats dotted the shoreline reminding him that he'd better check in with Bill about the race before he got lost doing too much more dreaming over Saddie. But, afterward, Damon thought, he was going to show Saddie that he was not the man she thought he once was. He had changed. And he was ready for love.

****

Sabrina clutched at the red-checkered table cloth which was wrapped around the registration table. The wind had really picked up in the last hour. She held down the boat registration papers to keep them from lifting off and sailing into the waters. Grey clouds covered the sky, and white caps churned in the water. The storm came up quickly. In a matter of minutes, the rain would pelt down onto the table and soak them. A number of boats were turning and coming back to the land—forfeiting the race in return for safety. Sabrina scanned the horizon. Damon was out there somewhere. Would his skipper turn the boat around or would he insist they could sail through anything? She fought the panic rising in her chest as she remembered another storm and sailing race. The other storm which had taken another man away from her.

"You okay?" Cassie asked beside her.

"I'm fine," Sabrina insisted. She tried to push back her rising fears. Everything would be fine.

"You look kinda pale," Cassie said.

Sabrina pointed to the horizon where the thick dark clouds had stirred up the waters into large, white waves. She covered her mouth as her stomach gave a sharp heave.

"He's an experienced sailor," Cassie squeezed Sabrina's arm. "He'll be okay."

For a minute, both women watched as the boats tilted and heeled. From a distance, it looked as though the boats would tip right into the dark and stormy waves.

"Cassie! Sabrina" Elizabeth Atkins barked. "I need some help. We've got to get the tent down before it blows away."

Sabrina jumped to her feet, and holding onto the metal pole, leaned her weight against it as the wind threatened to blow it the other way. Papers from the registration table scattered in the wind. "Never seen anything like it," Elizabeth muttered as she yanked hard on the stake and pulled the tent to the ground. "Not in the middle of summer."

Sabrina's stomach tightened. Was she going to lose a second man to the storms of the waters? Sabrina watched, as Damon's boat continued to make its way out towards the starting line. She pointed, but the words froze in her throat.

"The fools." Elizabeth swore under her breath. "There's always a couple of them who don't listen. Think they can play with the storm. They'll get out there and race each other to their deaths." Elizabeth glanced at Sabrina's green face. "I'm sorry, dear," She patted her arm. "I forgot."

Sabrina could barely breathe as she watched the sailboat dip and roll in the waves. Damon was on that boat. Clutching her hands together, Sabrina felt like her world was exploding. It was far worse this time than when he'd left her at eighteen, because this time she knew, he'd come back to give her a second chance, and she'd been caught in her memories of the past. She hadn't been able to look past what happened at eighteen to the man he'd become. She hadn't even given him a chance. Like the boat sailing into the storm, she'd been the one to sail back into the storm. This time, she'd been the foolish one.

****

The wind blew hard around Damon as he adjusted the jib. Storms never scared him. He'd sailed in the roughest waters. Bill's cheeks were flushed red with excitement and his eyes glowed. "Big one out there." Bill pointed to the white caps crashing on the waters. "Knock a few people out of the race."

Damon nodded to Bill and reached for a yellow wet jacket. He made sure the line around his waist was tied on tight—harnessing him to the boat. In the distance, Damon could see boats turning around and calling it quits—even before the Regatta had started. On shore, the crowd lined the pier. He squinted. Was she there? Was Saddie watching? As a teenager, they'd spent many nights on the pier, eating ice cream, wrapped in each other's arms and watching the boats as they sailed in from summer Regattas. Although, he'd been too young to understand, there was nothing better than those nights.

Nothing.

"Turn it around!" Damon called over the storm.

"What?" Bill hollered over the crashing waves as he tried to hold onto the boat's ruder.

"Turn it around!" Damon yelled louder. Sailing into the storm was something he might have done as a younger man. A younger man who didn't care if he lived or died, and wanted to prove he could outrun any storm. But all that had changed the minute he saw Saddie again. He had a life he wanted. A woman he needed. And he wasn't going to ruin that life by trying to outrun a storm.

****

An hour later, Sabrina circulated among the sailors sprawled out on the plush couches and chairs in the living room. She poured another cup of coffee and turned towards the kitchen to check on a large pot of soup. The sailors had poured into the Bed and Breakfast when the Regatta ended. Once they'd dried, and gotten a little shot of brandy in them, the room turned into a festive party. And if she wasn't so worried about Damon, Sabrina would have allowed herself to enjoy the party atmosphere. But she couldn't concentrate on anything. Why hadn't he come back? Why wasn't he sitting around with the other sailors telling stories and winking at her? Why was she so cold to him earlier in the day? And even worse, why hadn't she just given in to what her heart was telling her? She loved him. She'd always loved Damon. It was only her stubborn nature that refused to allow her to surrender to him.

Setting the coffee pot on the warmer in the living room, a movement outside the picture window caught her eye. Looking towards the shed, Sabrina noticed the door was ajar. The rain had been coming down for an hour now. The shed would be soaking. Frustrated with herself that she'd left the door open, Sabrina headed out into the pelting rain without grabbing her jacket. Immediately, she was soaked. Reaching the shed, Sabrina paused. A small light glowed from inside. Candle light.

Sabrina paused. Was her niece, Caitlin inside? Had Caitlin decided to use the opportunity for time with her boyfriend? She wanted to give Caitlin space. She knew all too well what it was like being a teenager and in love. But, what if it wasn't Caitlin inside? What if an animal managed to work its way into her shed? Sabrina shuddered. She didn't want to think of the mess a raccoon could leave. No, she steeled herself. She had to find out who or what was inside.

Sabrina pushed open the door and exhaled softly. The shed had been lit with small globe candles. A bottle of wine with two glasses sat on the small table. It wasn't a raccoon.

Damon sprawled across the bed. His hand was splayed across his face. His eyes were closed and he looked pale and exhausted.

Stepping close to him, Sabrina's heart contracted. The storm had not claimed him. He'd come back. And this time she was not going to be foolish. She was not going to let her pride and fears of the past get in the way. Being careful not to wake him, Sabrina pulled out a thick comforter from the old wood trunk at the end of the bed. It had been her Grandmother's, and when she was cold or sick, Grandma always covered her in the blanket. Sabrina gently laid the blanket across Damon's outstretched body.

"Saddie," He murmured. Damon reached out and took hold of her hand.

Saddie sank to the bed and let Damon pull her gently down beside him. She stretched out beside him, and immediately felt her body sigh. She'd come home.

Shifting, Damon arranged the blanket so it was wrapped over the two of them before he gently encircled her in his arms. "I was waiting for you."

Saddie leaned over and softly placed her warm lips on his. "I've been waiting for you too."

Love's Bid

"You sent letters to everyone?" Cassie inhaled sharply.

"Yes." Eric's right eye-brow arched upward. His voice dropped an octave to a smooth rolling drawl. "I thought that's what we agreed at the last Board Meeting. Everyone had a strong application and all should be funded." Dark curly hair framed Eric's face. His sharp, crystal- clear blue eyes took most women's breath away. But Cassie was not swayed by Eric's looks or his charm. She'd been his high school girlfriend and the boy she'd once loved, never grew up. This incident was just another one of Eric's escapades.

A light spring wind blew through the open window of the board room. From the marina below, the sailboat's masts tinkled like wind chimes.

"I'm so glad that we funded everyone," Elizabeth said, and smiled. "I love watching the teens in the summer sailing camp regatta." She reached for a blueberry muffin from the blue and yellow paisley plate in the middle of the table. Her coral painted fingernails complimented her light pink lipstick. A silver bracelet slid up and down her tanned arm and matched small, silver hoop earrings.

"Young sailors make great crew!" Bill's voice rolled through the room in a rich and deep baritone. Cassie was reminded of her days crewing for Bill after college. Bill had a knack for taking high school and college men and women onto his boat and teaching them the ropes. Bill's sailors not only won regattas, but they also went on to successful careers in everything from banking to real estate to architecture. Bill never took any credit for the lessons. He simply showed up in the spring and asked for the next group of young people to fill his crew roster. A few more wrinkles lined Bill's face, and his sandy brown hair was completely gray, but the years on the water had maintained his lean, tall, frame.

Cassie rubbed her eyes. She enjoyed acting as the Sailing Club Foundation Board President, but, sometimes, she wondered if she spoke the same language as the rest of the Board. "Sadie? Damon?" Cassie turned to her left. She hoped someone remembered the conversation from last month.

Sadie frowned and flipped the stapled papers in front of her. The two-carat diamond ring on her left hand, caught in the sunlight. Damon had provided the best for his new wife. If the unmistakable sparkle in Sadie's eyes and color in her cheeks were any indication, married life agreed with her very well. Cassie felt happy for her best friend, but sometimes she missed the long hours they'd spent together since childhood.

"Damon?" Cassie asked. "Do you remember the last meeting?'

"Sorry," Damon said. "I think I was a little preoccupied last month." He gazed with tenderness at Sadie.

Cassie shook her head. They hadn't been able to fund every request. There had been too many applications and not enough donations from the Foundation's Annual Holiday Dinner Dance.

"I said," Cassie said slowly as she carefully looked around the table, "Everyone deserved to be funded. I did not say that it was possible to grant funds to all applicants. Now usually this wouldn't be a problem, but it seems Eric has taken it upon himself to send out letters granting funds to everyone." Cassie paced the front of the narrow room. "This means we will need to figure out a way to either retract those letters or to find funding." The headache pulsed between Cassie's eyes. She rubbed the back of her neck and felt the knots. It would take a couple of good massages to work out this tension.

If it'd been up to her, she would have removed Eric from the Board with his last escapade. It'd been Eric's job to provide the entertainment for the black tie dinner. Cassie assumed he'd find a band to play classical music. Instead, he'd hired a magician. To make matters worse, Eric hadn't bothered to check with her, or the hotel hosting the dinner. In a streak of bad timing, the magician released a pair of doves. The doves flew into the rafters of the hotel ballroom. At the same time, the Department of Health dropped in for a surprise visit. The hotel's owner was furious and denied the use of the hotel for further Sailing Foundation events. Cassie was mortified the Sailing Foundation received such a black mark on their name. She'd tried to explain to Eric it wasn't high school. They were board members for the city's prestigious Sailing Club Foundation. But Eric shrugged it off and said there were plenty of hotels in the city. They would find another one for future events.

Eric tapped his pen on the table. "We can't go back and tell the teens at the YMCA camp we don't have funding for their summer sailing program."

"That's exactly what we should do." Cassie snapped. "But," she softened as Sadie frowned and shook her head, "we will find a way to get the money." There was no way Cassie would ever dream of telling teens they didn't have funding. She remembered all too well her own teen years. She and Mom relied on the generosity of strangers to fund school supplies, camps, and winter coats. She'd gone more than one back-to-school season without new school supplies because donations were down. As an adult, she vowed never to disappoint young people who depended on her. The grant program was one of the reasons Cassie loved her position as the Sailing Foundation Board's President. She loved seeing the teen sailors at the sailing camp given an opportunity to experience something which otherwise might never have been possible. "You got us into this mess," Cassie said to Eric. "What do you propose we do?"

"An auction." Eric leaned back in his chair, and with his feet planted firmly, he pushed two chair legs off the ground. The chair tottered, but Eric maintained balance. Cassie pressed her lips together. When she taught art in the elementary classes, she told the children to keep "all four on the floor." It took all her willpower not to tell Eric the same. It was just another way Eric acted like a child.

"What items will we auction?" Sadie asked. Her voice carried a hint of a smile. Sadie loved nothing more than a challenge—something she'd proven with her very successful Bed and Breakfast. She'd taken her business from nothing and built it into the most exclusive place to stay in the city.

Cassie crossed her arms and waited to hear how Eric would squirm his way out of this one. In high school, she'd been swayed by Eric's charm and persuasion. As Art Club Advisor, she'd met Eric at a Student Government Council meeting. He'd been the class's Vice President and always seemed to have one grand scheme after another up his sleeve. Cassie was enthralled with being a part of Eric's exciting ideas. But the high school thrill- seeking wore thin during college. Cassie juggled long hours working as a waitress and attending classes. She didn't have enough energy to keep up with Eric. By the end of her first year of college, they'd gone their separate ways. Cassie hadn't seen Eric again until he'd joined the Sailing Foundation Board.

"We can auction sailors." Eric scanned the faces at the table. "I think we've got quite a crew who'd be great on the auction block." He placed his left hand on the table and pushed further back in his chair. Cassie waited for him to topple to the ground, but, somehow, he managed to hold his balance.

"I love it!" Sadie exclaimed. She leaned over and kissed Damon on the cheek. "I'd pay a pretty price for you."

Damon squeezed Sadie's hand. He whispered something in her ear which caused her cheeks to flush.

"Sailors?" Cassie sputtered. She did not want the Sailing Foundation Auction to be a sex auction. She was the President of the Foundation's Board, and she was a respected artist in the city. She'd been hired for commissioned pieces by some of the city's wealthiest residents. When she didn't work as an artist, she ran a successful school art program and volunteered her time in many city events. Cassie did not need to have her name associated with some risqué event nor did any of the other board members.

"I don't think..." she began.

"It will be an auction of a service provided by the sailors." Eric interrupted. "Not an auction of sailors." He winked at Cassie.

Cassie flushed and turned away from Eric. She busied herself with pouring a large cup of coffee from the pot on the table. Eric knew just what she thought and how to find the exact buttons to cause a reaction. Cassie dumped a huge heaping of sugar into her coffee, and took a drink. She was not going to let Eric bother her. This wasn't high school. She wasn't his girlfriend anymore. She did not need to let him affect her. Cassie slowly turned around to face Eric. She pasted a bland smile on her face and nodded at him. "What exactly are you thinking?" she asked, hoping that her voice conveyed an air of utter detachment.

"The sailors will each donate a service," Eric said. "A handyman service, painting, or taking families for a picnic on their boats. We can advertise it, not just to the sailors and their families, but to the entire city."

"Great idea!" Bill said. "The auction will introduce the community to sailing. We might even find a few people who want to be sailors!"

"It is a good idea," Elizabeth said softly. Her eyes glowed as she gazed at Bill. Everyone could see that Elizabeth was hopelessly in love with Skipper Bill. Something which, Cassie thought sadly, Bill had yet to notice.

Cassie paced the room. Auctions weren't a bad thing. They could be a lot of work, but they did bring in a great deal of money. If they stayed away from an

"Fine." Cassie said. "I'll offer a personalized garden art bench. Does that satisfy you?"

"Perfect." Eric didn't take his eyes from Cassie. "You're not worried about the bidding are you?"

"No." Cassie reddened. "Why would I be?"

"I don't know." Eric drawled. "It just seems a little chilly in this room and you're sweating."

Flustered, Cassie reached up and wiped a small band of sweat away from her forehead.

"I am sweating over your decision to send out the funding letters."

Eric tossed back his head and laughed loudly. "You've got a keen sense of humor, Cassie. You always have."

Cassie met Eric's eyes. For a minute, she saw herself as a teenage girl who was in love with her fun, charming boyfriend. She remembered the hours they spent at the marina. They always sat on the bow of various boats that didn't belong to them. When she'd protest they were trespassing, Eric would say that no one would mind. He'd pull her closer, whisper in her ears, and kiss her until the world stopped and all she could think of was the two of them. Together. Forever.

Dreams.

All childish dreams.

***

Outside the marina's bar and grill, Eric leaned against the concrete wall. He flipped through the texts on his phone. A family crisis—again.

Eric punched in his sixteen-year-old nephew Devon's phone number. He refused to text. The phone barely rang before Devon answered.

"What's going on?" Eric snapped.

Devon's voice tumbled into Eric's left ear in a rush. A group of them tagged the bridge by the rail yards. The police showed up. Devon ran. The police didn't catch him. Could he just pop by Eric's office and hang out for a bit? Maybe throw them off trail?

"No," Eric said curtly. "I'll meet you and we'll go down to the police station. You can turn yourself in. I will not harbor a criminal. I'll meet you at the house in fifteen minutes."

Eric hung up the phone and pocketed it. He clenched his fists and fought back a surge of hot anger. He'd taken Devon into his home six months ago when his sister went to jail for drug trafficking. No one had heard from Devon's dad for years. Eric tried to give Devon jobs. He wanted the boy to learn responsibility, but every one of the jobs ended in disaster. The last was the Foundation Funding letters. It was a simple job.

Eric showed Devon the two files on his computer. There was a list of names for people who would receive funding as well as a list of names of those who would not receive money. But, somehow, Devon misunderstood the directions and sent approval letters to everyone.

Eric thought he did well to cover the tracks at the Board Meeting. He'd been shocked to hear Cassie announce that everyone received funding letters, but years of getting caught off- guard by his sister's behavior taught him to cover his tracks well. Growing up, Eric spent years covering his sister's drug use and continual jail stints with a smooth charm which distracted most people. He learned how to draw people close enough to see some of him, but not all. The only person he'd ever felt close enough to trust was Cassie. But he'd never been able to tell her about his sister. Rebecca was six years older than him, and for as long as Eric could remember, she'd gotten in trouble. By the time Eric reached high school, Rebecca's drug use had escalated and the fun, older sister he'd once loved had become a monster.

When Eric sat with Cassie on the boats at the marina, he wanted to tell Cassie how it felt to listen to his Mom pace the floor at night. He wanted to tell her how it felt to sit at the breakfast table and wait for the knock on the door or the phone call from the police. He wanted to tell Cassie about the Saturday mornings they'd driven over to the jail and spent two hours sitting in the visitor's waiting room listening to Rebecca say it was everyone's fault but hers.

But it'd never seemed like the right time. Cassie knew him as a happy-go-lucky boy. If he'd changed, she might not like that person. When they got to college, Cassie got so serious and Eric didn't know what to do. By that point, he'd created so many lies about his life he didn't know how to change from the happy-go-lucky boy everyone loved to a man who knew how to be honest. The four years of college flew by in an endless stream of parties and girls, and when he graduated, Eric found himself with a job working for a financial firm. The father of a girl he was dating set up the job, with the hope that Eric might soon become a son-in-law. Eric never became a son-in-law, but he'd used his charm to work his way up the corporate ladder.

It was his father's heart attack and his sister's six-year jail sentence that brought Eric back to Rochester. He found a new position at a financial office in the city and used his success to buy a large lake home with a carriage house. His father survived the heart attack, but the medical bills ate up his parent's retirement.

Eric moved his parents into the carriage house, and when his sister went to jail, opened his house to Devon. When the girls Eric knew in high school called him to go to dinner, he turned them down. He wasn't a sixteen-year-old charming boy who everyone loved anymore. He was a man with responsibilities.

One day, not long after he'd moved back, Eric found a set of beautifully painted benches at a local garden shop. He immediately recognized Cassie's colorful style. The shop owner said Cassie had become quite well-known and respected in the city. She'd offered a way to contact Cassie, but Eric declined. Cassie had done very well for herself. The last thing Eric wanted to do was upset her by falling into his life with all his family problems.

He would have kept that promise to stay away from Cassie, but one night, after Eric was home about a month, Bill took Eric out sailing. Bill mentioned the Treasury position was open on the Sailing Club Foundation Board. Eric protested he wasn't a member of the Sailing Club, but Bill waved Eric's excuses away and told him that was easy to fix with the swipe of a pen and a check which would reinstate his membership.

Bill mentioned Cassie was the Board's President, and Eric found himself pulling out his checkbook and writing the membership check. Attending Board Meetings with Cassie couldn't harm. They'd be surrounded by the other Board members and focused on the task at hand. Eric could be around Cassie without coming close to disrupting the life she'd made with the disaster of the life his had become. It seemed like the perfect plan.

"Excuse me." A young girl who worked at the bar and grill stood in front of Eric. She held a platter and notepad. Her blonde hair was tied up in a ponytail and framed a heart-shaped face. Small freckles danced across her cheeks and nose. "Can I get you something?"

"No thanks," Eric said. "Not right now." He smiled at her. Eric remembered the first year of college and how hard Cassie worked. He remembered the large black circles under Cassie's eyes, and the smile that never quite reached her eyes. When he stopped by to visit, Cassie tried to stay engaged with him, but leaned on the diner counter as if she just wanted to lie down and sleep for a long time. There was so much he could have done to support her in those college years. But he'd been a boy and he let Cassie drift away from him.

Now, Eric thought, he wanted to make things up to her. He wanted to show Cassie who he'd become as an adult, but the first thing he had to do was deal with Devon.

***

Cassie drove her silver Toyota through the black wrought iron gates and up the circular driveway. Carefully, she angled the car past the large, three-story brick house and pulled to a stop in front of a small carriage house. The year after her mom died, she rented a carriage house like this one. That year, Cassie found peace sitting in front of a crackling fire and staring out onto the water. She worked on a few paintings, but most of the year, she spent time watching the changing seasons on the lake. At times, her grief overpowered her and she wished for siblings to share the loss. But, for as long as Cassie could remember, there had been no one but Mom and her.

Turning off the ignition, Cassie slipped her car keys into her orange-and- red summer shoulder bag. She'd been proud at finding the shoulder bag. It'd been a garage sale find she picked up for a dollar. Most of her clothing came from thrift stores or garage sales. She learned to save money as a child and it worked to her advantage as an artist with a limited household budget.

Cassie rolled down the car window and inhaled the cool breeze from the lake. She stared, mesmerized, into the blue waters. It'd been over five years since Mom passed away and Cassie learned to fill her time, especially holidays, with friends and neighbors. Cassie smiled as she thought of her neighbor, Lucy Blackwillow. Cassie spent many evenings reading or watching late-night movies with Lucy. Lucy's daughter and son-in-law lived in Florida with their three children, and although they wanted Lucy to move and live with them, Lucy refused to go. Secretly, Cassie was glad. She didn't know what she would do if Lucy moved away. Cassie loved brewing a pot of tea and curling up under an old patchwork quilt to watch old movies or read books with Lucy. At night, Cassie always made sure to check on Lucy before she went to bed. Cassie would peer out her bedroom window and up at Lucy's window. A few minutes later, Lucy lifted the curtains and waved before lowering the blind for the night. Cassie liked to pretend Lucy was the Grandmother she didn't have.

Cassie smoothed her hands over her pastel skirt. She checked her hair in the rearview mirror and straightened a stray curl. Quickly, Cassie double-checked the address she'd hastily scrawled on the back of her hand. 723 Lakeview Road. She was at the right place. Cassie swallowed and licked her lips. She exited the car, shut the door firmly behind her and walked up the brick walkway.

Blooming purple lilacs and colorful red and yellow tulips danced merrily in a soft breeze coming off the lake. Someone had a flair for gardening. Cassie climbed four stone steps leading to an impressive three-story brick house. The black door matched the shutters and a small gold plate etched with the last name of "Atkins" hung above the gold doorbell.

Cassie pressed hard on the doorbell and waited. Her stomach roiled with small butterflies. In the flurry of planning for the auction, she'd overlooked the most important part—securing the procurement forms. And that, Sadie had explained to her, was something only Eric could do as Board Treasurer. It wasn't like her to be so careless, but there had been too much on her plate for months. First, there was the auction for the school district, then there was the children's spring art camp, and then a large order came in for her painted mural benches. She'd been working frantically, night and day.

The hard work obviously affected her ability to concentrate.

Cassie stepped back and stared upward at the massive house. Eric had done very well for himself. All his schemes must have come to something, she mused.

A metal shovel hitting the sidewalk caused Cassie to jump, turn around and meet up face-to-face with Eric. She breathed deeply and took in his blue jeans covered with dirt, a deep wet line of sweat running down his black T-shirt, and a long narrow band of dirt across crossed his forehead.

"Cassie." Eric frowned. "Did we have a meeting?"

Cassie's mouth parted slightly, but the words didn't form.

"Cass?" Eric repeated.

"The auction." Cassie fumbled in her bag. "I need to go over the list of sailors and their items with you. We need procurement forms. I'm sorry to barge in on you at home, but we don't have much time. I didn't want to wait until our next board meeting."

"Oh." Eric cleared his throat. He leaned back on the shovel. His long tapered fingers tapped the handle. "The auction."

Was it her imagination or did Eric seem disappointed? No, she thought. It was only her lack of sleep, the last three nights, getting to her. She felt delusional.

Cassie grabbed a manila folder from her bag. She opened it to the list of sailor's names. It wasn't as long as she had hoped, but with a good amount of high bids, they should be able to pull off a successful auction. A sudden gust of wind from the lake blew the papers onto the walk-way. Cassie leaned down to scoop them up, and as she did, her barrette slipped and her hair cascaded around her shoulders. Cassie sighed and yanked her hair back up into place. When she looked up, a look crossed Eric's face she couldn't quite read. Her eyes held his as he reached out and moved a strand of stray hair away from her cheek.

"Thanks." Cassie muttered. "Sometimes things just fly away from me." She didn't take her eyes from his. His fingers played with her hair.

"Sorry." Eric cleared his throat and yanked his hand away as if it'd been bitten. "Come around back to the deck. It's more protected from the wind."

Cassie's heart pounded as she followed Eric. She would not let herself get swept away with feelings for him. It didn't matter how incredibly good he looked in his work jeans, or how his eyes sought out hers in a dance that ached with the promise of long sensual nights.

Cassie slowly trailed behind Eric. She couldn't help but notice the colorful beds of red and orange dahlias and purple lilacs. "The gardens are beautiful. You must have a wonderful gardener."

Eric stopped abruptly and turned to face her. "I do the gardening."

Cassie inhaled, took a small step backwards and stumbled. Eric smelled like dirt and a musky aftershave. It took all her willpower not to step forward, lean against him, and surrender to his charms.

"Careful." Eric placed his hand on Cassie's arm. "A couple of the path's stones stick out the wrong way. It's easy to catch yourself."

Cassie steadied herself, but felt as if her insides were falling away. Eric's deep, rich brown eyes gazed down at her.

"Gardening is different than working with numbers, I imagine." Cassie murmured. She couldn't quite catch her breath. Small flecks of gold danced in Eric's warm brown eyes, and tiny wrinkles crinkled at the edges. She fought the urge to reach up and run her fingers over the small freckles on his cheeks.

"Yes." Eric's voice caught deep in his throat. His eyes drifted lower to Cassie's lips and then back up to her eyes. "Gardening is different than numbers."

The wind from the lake whipped across Cassie's hot checks. She tried to take a deep breath. She had to pull herself together. She had a job.

Cassie forced herself to turn away from Eric and toward the backyard. A 35-foot sailboat was docked at the foot of the sloping backyard. She could see the name etched across the back—Pelican II. Large, colorful hanging baskets hung from the rafters of a wrap-around porch. A petite woman sat at a wrought iron table.

"I didn't know you had company." Cassie flushed. "I really should go. We can do this another time."

"You remember my mom," Eric said, and smiled.

"Your mom?" Cassie could barely remember meeting Eric's mom. In high school, she'd spent very little time at Eric's house. He'd insisted that privacy at his house was an issue. But now, doubt played at the edges of her mind. Why did Eric always want to spend time at her house and not his? Why hadn't she met his mom more than one or two times? They had dated for two years— more than enough time to know the mom of the boy she loved. The few times she'd asked about his family, Eric always said that his mom volunteered at the hospital gift shop or practiced in the church choir, his Dad worked, and his sister attended community college. Eric made it seem like everyone was busy but him. Had Eric been covering something up? Was there more to Eric than she'd known?

"Does your mom still live in the house where you grew up?" Cassie asked politely, hoping that Eric's answer might give her some clue into his family secrets.

"Mom and Dad live in the guesthouse. Mom likes the afternoon sun on the porch. Dad likes his nap on the couch in front of a good baseball game," Eric chuckled. "Can't say I blame him."

"Baseball?" Cassie tilted her head upward. "I didn't know you liked baseball."

"Something I picked up in college."

"Oh," Cassie said, suddenly remembering how much she had wanted and needed Eric in college and how he had disappointed her. The ache in her chest reminded her not to become too enamored with Eric.

"Good afternoon!" Jessica's sunny voice carried over the yard. She waved to Eric and Cassie. Jessica's manicured red nail polish matched her lipstick and the

Romance for all the Seasons

red flowers in her sundress. Cassie licked her lips. She should have put on a little more lipstick. She never remembered to wear lipstick unless she attended an art opening. Cassie slipped her hands into her pockets. It was always so hard to remove paint from her nails.

"Please, have a seat," Jessica said. "There are plenty of chairs. Eric always tells me he's going to have a party. But no one ever shows up. You're the first!"

Cassie peeked at Eric from the corner of her eye. This didn't sound like the Eric she'd once known, or the one she'd seen at the Board Meetings. Eric always had people around him. His life was a constant party.

"I don't have time." Eric replied abruptly. He snapped a dead geranium flower from one of the large pots on the porch, and pushed away a spot of dirt on the porch step with his foot.

Jessica shook her head. "He works too hard."

"He's very good with numbers." Cassie defended Eric. She walked across the porch to the wrought iron table. Her artist eyes took in every detail of the yard. Purple and white lilac bushes bordered the perfectly manicured lawn. Large sunflowers and lavender bushes filled spacious flower beds. Tiny gnome statues peeked from between the flowers. Cassie smiled. She'd rarely seen a garden so full of life and yet, at the same time, having such an air of playfulness. Just like Eric, Cassie thought as she spotted a small area in the far corner of the yard that begged for one of her specialized benches.

"I don't know what we would have done without him," Jessica said. "Mark has had with some health issues. All of the bills ate away at our retirement. If it hadn't been for Eric, we would have been out on the street."

"Mom." Eric quickly stepped up on the porch and stood behind Jessica. He squeezed her shoulders gently.

"Don't mind me." Jessica waved away Eric's attention. She smiled at Cassie. "There's a pitcher of lemonade. I can get glasses for both of you."

"I'll get them." Cassie searched the porch for an outdoor cabinet. She'd discovered, in her year of living in the carriage house, that houses on the lake kept outdoor utensils and plates in a cabinet on the deck. It was easier to entertain guests.

Suddenly, the back porch door banged open. A boy, who looked to be about sixteen, thundered onto the porch. He carried a bag of potato chips in his left hand and texted into a cell phone with his right. His thick dark hair cascaded over his long, narrow face, and his arms and legs stretched forever.

Cassie paused. Did Eric have a son? She hadn't heard that Eric married or had a child, but Cassie began to suspect there was a lot Eric kept hidden.

"Rick says they're going to let us off easy." The boy waved his cell phone at Eric. "We just gotta show up for the court date next Friday. The railroad isn't going to press charges for the tagging."

Cassie whirled around and studied the teen. She often worked with kids in juvenile detention as an art mentor. Most of the kids were very creative and they just needed a little guidance and structure. Cassie wondered if this boy might be someone who could work with her. The probation officers usually did a good job matching the kids. Each week, Cassie spent a few hours meeting with the teens in a large classroom in the detention center. Cassie brought the necessary art supplies, and, as they worked on a simple drawing or painting, they talked about life as an artist.

"We're not discussing this now," Eric growled. He walked up to the boy and yanked the cell phone from his hands. "Cassie, meet Devon. Devon, this is Cassie."

"Hey." With a non-committal shrug, Devon waved his right hand at Cassie and said to Eric. "Can I have my phone back, please?"

"No." Eric pocketed the cell. He handed Devon the shovel he'd been carrying. "The bed by the driveway needs to be weeded and the dead plants removed."

Devon took the shovel and stepped off the porch. "Nice to meet you." He hollered over his shoulder and headed toward the side of the porch.

"You too." Cassie replied truthfully.

Eric cleared his throat and shuffled his feet. "Sorry about that. If you want to reschedule a time when I can meet you in the office, I understand. It's a little chaotic around here."

"No," Cassie said quickly. "Now is perfect." She gently placed her right hand on Eric's forearm. There was a lot more going on at Eric's house than she'd ever dreamed possible. And, in the last fifteen minutes, she'd realized she hadn't given Eric a chance to show her who he'd become as an adult. Now, she wanted to see if there was a man inside the boy she'd once known and loved. "I have all afternoon. If someone can just tell me where I might find a glass for the lemonade. It looks delicious."

"In the kitchen, dear," Jessica called. "Open the door and turn to your left. Look in the first cabinet on the left."

Cassie turned and pulled the sliding glass door open. She stepped into a kitchen three times the size of her cottage. She inhaled sharply, and, pretending she'd visited at Eric's estate house often, Cassie headed for the first cabinet on her left.

***

Two hours later, Eric lifted the steaming pan of chicken enchiladas from the oven. He placed the glass dish on the granite countertop. Cassie trailed behind him carrying two ceramic plates. Outside the large kitchen windows, the sun sparkled on the lake and a small group of seagulls floated in the water.

Eric couldn't remember the last time he'd spent such an enjoyable afternoon. He liked hearing the sound of Cassie's voice float through the house as she continued to call the sailors. She'd been relentless with some and charming with others. And, by the end of the afternoon, there was a long list of names and procurement forms ready to be signed. "Who else is coming?" Eric motioned toward the stack of plates and grinned at her.

"Your Mom, Dad, Devon, me, you." Cassie ticked the names off on her fingers.

Eric shook his head. "Mom and Dad won't eat with us. They are on special diets. Devon needs to be somewhere else." Suddenly, Eric cleared his throat. He didn't want to tell Cassie that Devon would be attending a court-ordered youth class for three hours. He wanted her to think of him as the carefree, happy-go-lucky boy. It wouldn't work to dump all his family problems on her right away.

"Oh." Cassie looked down at the plates and back up at him. A smile broke across her face. "Then, I guess we don't need all these plates, do we?" Quickly, she picked up all the plates but two, and turning, opened the white kitchen cabinet and placed the plates back inside. "Problem solved."

"I guess it probably looked as though I was feeding an army." Eric felt the need to clarify himself. He waved his hand across the steaming pan of chicken enchiladas. "I just like to make a lot of food when I cook. I freeze it for lunch."

"Good idea." Cassie took the silver spatula Eric held up for her and their fingers touched. "I always end up eating the box meals for lunch. I never think to cook at night. I get too lost in some project, and then before I know it, it's too late to make some dinner. Mmmm..." Cassie took a bite of enchilada. A thin piece of cheese hung off her chin.

Eric reached over, and very slowly, lifted the piece of cheese from her lower jaw. She gazed up at him. His eyes dropped to her lips. With his right hand, Eric took Cassie's plate from her and very slowly, leaned down and placed his lips on Cassie's. He moved his lips gently against hers and felt them warm under his. Her mouth parted and a small sigh escaped her.

Cassie pressed against him and he leaned against the kitchen counter. His arms encircled her as he pulled her close to him. The warmth of the kitchen merged with the heat between them. He deepened the kiss. Cassie's fork clattered to the ground.

Eric slid his hands down Cassie's back, encircling and rubbing. The stove timer beeped and he reached around Cassie, fumbling for the button to shut it off.

Swiftly, Cassie slipped her arm around him and silenced the timer. "Happens all the time."

Eric bent down, picked up Cassie's fork and dropped it into the sink. He pulled open a drawer beside him and grabbed up a clean one. "Forks on the floor happen all the time, too."

Cassie laughed. She picked up her plate and carried it out to the porch. A small fire in the porch fire pit glowed brightly in the twilight. Fireflies darted around the yard sending off small flickers of light.

"Do you remember when we caught the fireflies?" Cassie asked as she settled back in her chair.

"Of course." Eric said, and chuckled. "We had that science project, but no one wanted to kill the fireflies. After baseball practice, we convinced Coach Anderson to let us into the building and we stuck all the jars in our bags and released them."

Eric smiled fondly. The releasing of the fireflies was a senior prank which turned out well. The next day, the lab was called off and not one person said a word about what happened to the fireflies.

A dark weight descended on Eric's chest as he stared into the crackling fire. That was also the day when everything fell apart. He arrived home to find his sister arrested for drugs. It was the beginning for her of years spent in and out of the court system—something which continued to this day.

"Eric." Cassie touched Eric's hand. "Is something the matter?"

Eric shook his head. The words lodged in his throat. He wanted to tell Cassie. He wanted to tell her everything. He wanted to tell her about his sister, and Devon, and how it felt to carry his family's responsibilities, but he couldn't make the words form. Instead, he flippantly leaned back in his chair, and, pushing two legs off the ground, said, "Life is good, isn't it?"

Cassie blanched, and Eric realized his mistake. Cassie wasn't some naïve high school girl. Cassie knew something was wrong and that he wasn't telling her.

"I think I should go," Cassie said without looking at Eric. "I've got a busy day ahead of me."

"Me too," Eric mumbled. "We got a lot done today."

"Yes," Cassie said slowly. "We did."

She looked up at him, and in her eyes, Eric saw the pain reflected there— pain he'd caused by his inability to let her know how he truly felt and who he truly was. He'd shown her one side of himself, and then just when she'd gotten close, he'd put up a wall. He was unable to allow her to see anymore. He'd become so good at presenting a superficial side that he didn't know how to show anything else. The best thing to do, Eric thought, was to make sure Cassie never had to deal with any more pain. The easiest way to do that was to remove himself from her life.

***

Cassie waited behind the stage. The auction had gone very well. They were only half-way through, and already, there was easily enough money to fund all of the requests this year as well as into next year. At this rate, the Foundation would be able to double their funding requests for the next three years.

Cassie shifted nervously on her left foot and then her right.

Sadie hugged her. "Ready for your big moment?"

"Of course," Cassie said, and tried to smile. She tucked her sweating palms into the pockets of her skirt and tried to push back the feeling of wanting to throw up. It was more than the auction causing her fits of panic. Would Eric show up at the auction?

The last time she'd seen him was the afternoon at his house. He hadn't attended any of the auction planning meetings. A few weeks later, he told everyone work kept was keeping him busy and completed his Board responsibilities by e-mail and fax.

Meanwhile, Cassie was assigned to work with Devon at the Art Detention Mentor Program. She hoped to see Eric pick up Devon or drop him off. But, when she asked Devon, he waved a bus pass and said Eric wanted him to learn how to ride public buses. Devon did, however, enlighten Cassie about a few other things. And, as Cassie learned about Eric's sister and the responsibilities he carried for his family, her heart ached. Eric was far from the happy-go-lucky boy she'd known and he tried to present at the Board Meeting. Eric's leaving was because he was trying to hide from everyone—especially her.

"Our next sailor is offering a personalized garden bench." The auctioneer boomed. "Cassie Richardson, come on out."

Cassie pushed back the thick, red velvet curtains and stepped onto the stage. The lights were up high. She couldn't see beyond the first two rows, but she could tell by the applause that every seat in the auditorium was filled.

"Cassie's artistic talents are well-known in this area. She teaches youth art classes, mentors teens in the court art mentor program and is highly sought after for commissioned pieces." Cassie barely listened as the brief blurb was read. Her stomach pitched and rolled as if she was high on a Ferris wheel and looking straight down.

"Let's start the bidding at one-hundred dollars. Do I hear one-hundred?"

Cassie's heart pounded. The room was deadly quiet for the number of people who'd purchased auction tickets.

The auctioneer didn't miss a beat. "One-hundred! Do I hear one-hundred dollars?"

Lucy's voice echoed loudly. "One-hundred!"

"No." Cassie stepped forward. Lucy barely had enough money to cover her food and medicine. Cassie bought Lucy a ticket to the auction and gave it to her as a gift. She never expected Lucy to bid on her.

"One-hundred dollars!" The auctioneer boomed. "Do I hear one-fifty?"

"Five-hundred." Damon called from the left of the stage.

"Five hundred!" The auctioneer said.

"Six-fifty!" Sadie clamored.

"No." Cassie whispered miserably. These were her friends bidding. This was not how the auction was supposed to go. She'd rather have no bids than be pacified by her friend's bids.

"Five-Thousand!" A deep male voice said from the right side of the room.

Cassie raised her hand to shield her eyes. She tried to see into the darkness. The stage lights blinded her. She couldn't see beyond the first two rows.

" Five-Thousand!" The auctioneer said. "That's a serious bidder. Going once. Going twice."

"Sold! For five-thousand dollars!"

Cassie's hands shook. She turned and pushed her way through the red velvet curtains. Her legs threatened to give way beneath her as she slipped off her auction number and dropped it on a small table. "Excuse me." Cassie pushed through the sailors waiting their turn. She slipped out through the door that opened to the outside.

Cassie hurried around to the front of the auditorium. She opened the side door and stepped back inside. It was going to be impossible to find him. The doors to the theater were open, and the next sailor stood onstage. The bidding erupted into a chorus of voices as each bid rose higher and higher for the man's handyman service.

"Are you looking for me?" Eric stepped out of the shadows of the lobby.

"You bid on me?"

"They say," Eric said. "You have the best talent for garden benches. I have a garden that needs a bench."

"But why did you bid on me?" Cassie asked. "You could buy one of my benches at the garden shop."

"I love you, Cass," Eric said softly. He stared directly into her eyes. "There are things I needed to tell you, but I was afraid. I was afraid when you found out who I really was, you'd leave. It seemed better for me to leave than take the chance of showing you who I really was and having you reject me."

"Oh Eric." Cassie leaned against the wall for support. Her heart contracted and tears welled up in her eyes. "I love you. I love the real you. I love the you who is not afraid to show and tell me everything."

Eric stepped forward. He picked up a stray hair which had slipped out of Cassie's barrette and twirled it between his fingers. "Do you know the real item I bid on?"

"No."

"You."

"Me?" Cassie tossed back her head and laughed. "This isn't an auction of sailors," she said slyly and winked.

"Yes it is," Eric murmured as he lowered his lips to Cassie's. "And you are the sailor I will always bid on."

Halloween Love Fortune

"Romance is in your future." Sadie leaned over a green and turquoise crystal ball perched on a small wrought iron table. A black and gold scarf concealed Sadie's auburn hair. Her long, flowing black skirt draped to the white porch boards of the Elmheart Hotel. A creamy white peasant blouse gathered at the sleeves and a gold coin bracelet dangled from Sadie's slim wrist. "Someone will confess his love for you on Halloween night." Sadie leaned back in the white wicker porch chair. She moved a small pillow behind her back and shifted against it.

The wind rustled through orange and brown oak leaves, carried them along a curved front sidewalk and across the hotel's sweeping front yard toward Lake Ontario. It was almost four o'clock and the sun was already low in the sky. In another hour, darkness would arrive as well as the haunting ghouls and goblins of Halloween.

"I think your crystal ball is confused." Jenny carefully painted a white letter "B" on a small, rectangular wood board. Small splatters of white paint dotted her faded blue jeans. A red and white vintage apron covered her flannel shirt. A silver clasp held back her blonde shoulder-length hair from her round face.

Jenny looked up and smiled at her best friend, Sadie. "It's Halloween, not Valentine's Day."

"The fortune teller never lies," Hailey said and took a sip from a cup of steaming, hot apple cider. She placed the mug on a wicker table and pulled a heavy green cape tight around her short black skirt and black turtleneck. A tall witch hat moved askew on her thick, jet black curly hair. Hailey rocked gently in the white porch rocker.

"Fortunes are just for fun," Jenny said mildly. She dropped her paintbrush in a jelly jar of water. Jenny held the sign in front of her and studied the stenciled word, Haunted Barn. She wiped a spot of white paint away from the letter "H" and set the sign on the porch railing to finish drying.

"Halloween fortunes are magical," Hailey said. Her voice dropped an octave as if to convey the biggest secret in the world.

Jenny shook her head and laughed. Hailey sounded just like her ten-year-old daughter, Caitlin. Jenny met Hailey and Caitlin last spring at a Chamber of Commerce meeting. Hailey was present at the meetings as the newest owner of the Elmheart Hotel. As manager of Lake View Design and Showroom, Jenny often attended the chamber meetings. She enjoyed working with other business owners and often walked out with a new project or two. Children were not usually allowed at the chamber meetings, but

Caitlin convinced the members she needed to attend for a school project. She wanted to learn how businesses worked so she could help her classmates work on a spring fundraiser for their school.

At the meeting, Jenny sat next to Hailey and Caitlin. She was impressed with Hailey's strong vision for the Elmheart Hotel. As a child, Jenny often escaped to the spacious grounds of the Elmheart. She loved to hike through the overgrown trails and eat her picnic peanut butter sandwich. One day, Jenny followed a barn cat to her kittens and found Mr. Matthew painting a bookcase. Instead of becoming angry at Jenny for trespassing, Mr. Matthew invited her to help him. After that, Jenny often helped Mr. Matthew paint and fix up old pieces of furniture. She never said anything, but the Elmheart Hotel provided Jenny with a safe place— away from her parent's arguments.

Now, Jenny felt happy to see the hotel revived and come alive again under the new ownership of Hailey and her husband, Patrick. "The haunted barn is such a great idea," Jenny said. "I'm so glad we're all working on it together."

Sadie tapped her fake red nails against the ball. "I can't wait to give the Halloween fortunes." She picked up a small, metal bucket with a "donation" sign taped to the front. "We're going to raise a lot of money for the elementary school's new playground. Do you think I should tell people they are about to receive a lot of money? They might donate more."

Hailey's light laughter filled the porch. She adjusted her witch hat. "I really don't know what I would have done without both of you these last few months. Your ideas have all been wonderful. The hotel would never be ready for a party if it wasn't for you."

"I hope everything goes well. We've done a lot of work." Jenny gazed past Hailey and looked around the front porch. Strands of fake cobwebs hung from the rafter and small, golden lights dangled from the ceiling. Ghosts made out of old sheets, and stuffed with fabrics, hung from the ceiling. On the porch railings, black cat stenciled wood cut-outs hung by black ribbons. Three large silver tubs filled with shiny, red apples sat to the left of the front steps leading down to the yard. Barrels of hay lay scattered along the white picket fence and walkway that lead to the barn. The sounds of hammers and saws came from the barn as Hailey's husband, Patrick, and Sadie's husband, Damon, put the finishing touches on the haunted barn.

"Jenny did most of the work," Sadie said. "I've been too busy running the bed and breakfast to offer much help."

Jenny flushed at the compliment. She hoped to have her own showroom and spent many hours dreaming about filling orders based on a high demand for her creative design.

Inside the front entryway of the hotel, a grandfather clock chimed four o'clock. In just an hour, the Elmheart Hotel's first annual Halloween party would begin. It was the beginning of what would, hopefully, be the Elmheart's first successful holiday season. Although the rooms weren't open yet, the reservations had been pouring in for the Christmas holiday. It seemed everyone wanted to stay at the renovated hotel.

"It's almost the witching hour" Sadie said. "I'm so glad Halloween is not a big holiday at the bed and breakfast. It's nice to have a night off here and there." Sadie ran a successful Bed and Breakfast, but Jenny knew, in a few months when Sadie and Damon's twins arrived, Sadie's business could change. Jenny felt happy to see Sadie's life so full and happy. She had known Sadie since they were in community college together. During those years, Jenny struggled to support her sister and herself. Her mother passed away and her dad remarried and moved to Connecticut. After Mom died, Dad tried to convince Jenny to move with her sister, but Jenny felt her sister should finish high school in the small town where they both attended school all their lives. The house was paid for, so Jenny only needed enough money to cover the utilities and groceries every month. Jenny took a job waitressing and spent evenings attending the local community college. After she met Sadie in an accounting class, the

Jenny's warm hazel eyes met his. "Great. We're almost ready for the haunted barn." Jenny clapped her hands together. "It's very exciting."

Zach smiled at her enthusiasm. He loved Jenny's passion for her work. A spark danced in her eyes when she talked about a new idea or project. At night, as he got ready for work, he could hear her in the apartment above, walking back and forth as she moved between her computer and design table. Sometimes, on his patrol, he drove by their apartment building and saw her light glowing into the wee hours of the morning.

"The hotel reservations have been pouring in for the holiday season," Jenny continued. "We don't have much left to do on the guest rooms. It's just the main living room and sun porch that still need finishing."

Zach stuck his hands into his pockets and leaned back against the large barn door. Jenny never waited for things to happen. Zach had no doubt she would run her own decorating and design shop in a year or so. As soon as the Elmheart Hotel opened and everyone found out she created the design in the rooms, Jenny would be in high demand. It was only a matter of time before Jenny realized her friendship with him wouldn't satisfy her. She'd want something more. She would want a family of her own. Zach's heart twisted. But, family was something he couldn't give her—not with his job taking him out on the street into high criminal activity. It was one thing for him to take risks, but he could

113

never do it with a family to support. And he loved his job too much to give it up. The best thing for him was to remain unattached. Zach's heart leaped as he looked at Jenny. If he fell in love with someone, he didn't doubt that someone would be Jenny.

"Here it is!" Caitlin backed out of the backseat of the truck slowly. In her arms, she carried a round pumpkin.

"Caitlin!" Hailey scolded "That pumpkin doesn't look any different than the ones in the wagon. I really don't understand…"

"This pumpkin is very special," Caitlin said. Slowly, she walked toward Zach until she faced him. "This is your pumpkin to carve."

"Umpf," Zach said as he took the pumpkin from Caitlin. "I don't know if I'm very good at carving pumpkins." He turned to Jenny and winked at her. "How about you help me?"

Jenny's checks lightly flushed. "I don't know," she muttered. "I was going to…"

"Go on," Hailey said. "I've got to get back and finish up with the caramel apples for tonight. Patrick and Damon probably don't have much more to do with the barn set up. We can spare both of you for a little pumpkin carving."

"I've got a carving set." Caitlin bounced up and down on one foot and then the other. "It's on the porch." She looped her arm through Jenny's and yanked her toward the porch.

"Help me," Jenny turned and mouthed to Zach.

"I'm right behind you," Zach said, grinning as he followed Jenny and Caitlin up to the porch. It was always lively at the Elmheart Hotel and he loved spending his time there. In the last six months, Zach often volunteered to help Patrick with various yard projects. Zach enjoyed mowing the grass of the spacious lawn or raking leaves. The lake water sparkled in the sun and the outdoor work cleared his mind. Afterward, everyone gathered in the hotel's warm kitchen. Jenny was redecorating the rooms, and she and Hailey always joined them in the kitchen. Zach loved to listen to Jenny talk about her latest challenge or success as Patrick's soup simmered on the stove. Once Caitlin arrived home from school, her voice echoed up and down the hallway as Jenny's creative enthusiasm wrapped him in a warm cocoon of love. Zach knew the Elmheart Hotel would be a roaring success from the moment it opened.

When Caitlin and Jenny reached the hotel's front porch steps, Caitlin released Jenny's arm and headed for a small, blue backpack by the swing. Zach set the pumpkin down on a porch table while Hailey stepped inside and switched on the porch lamp. The porch filled with the light's warm glow and Zach took a step backward. He bumped against Jenny.

"Sorry," Zach mumbled, suddenly feeling like a nervous fourteen-year-old on a first date. He looked down at Jenny's illumined face tilted up to his. Zach couldn't take his eyes off her lush, pink lips. He wanted to lean over, take her in his arms and kiss her as if they had the best date of their lives.

"Here is the carving knife," Caitlin said.

Quickly, Zach pulled himself away from Jenny. He couldn't allow himself to go there. It wouldn't be fair to Jenny. He had to maintain control—just like he always did around her. He needed to act as though his feelings were only friendship.

"Where will we carve the pumpkin?" Jenny asked. "I think the porch table is too small to hold the weight."

"Sit," Caitlin directed. "Both of you can sit on the porch step."

"We must do as she says," Zach said, and without thinking, he grabbed Jenny's hand and pulled her down on the porch step beside him. Jenny leaned against him. Her familiar smell of lavender drifted around him, making him feel everything was right in the world.

Caitlin handed Jenny a small, plastic knife.

Jenny stared at the knife but did not take it from Caitlin.

"Caitlin!" Hailey called from inside the hotel. "I need help with the caramel apples."

116

"You'll have to do this yourself," Caitlin insisted. She dropped the plastic carving knife onto the porch and danced over to the screen door. "I love caramel apples." Without a backward glance at Jenny and Zach, Caitlin zipped inside the hotel.

"Jenny?" Zach reached over and picked up the carving knife. He turned the plastic knife over in his left hand. He doubted the knife would carve much of anything. It was no stronger than a plastic knife used at picnics. "What do you say? Can we carve this pumpkin?"

Jenny shook her head. "I'm sorry. I just don't think I've carved pumpkins since..." Jenny's voice broke off suddenly.

Zach's heart ached for her. Softly, he squeezed her hand. Zach wanted to tell Jenny nothing would ever harm her again. He knew her childhood hadn't been easy. She shouldered a lot of responsibility after her mom died. It hurt Jenny when her younger sister, Allison, married right out of high school, moved to San Diego and didn't invite Jenny to visit. Jenny had seen more than her share of heartache. Zach wanted nothing more than to take it all away and make sure she never hurt again. "We can do this together," Zach said, his voice husky with emotion. "Go ahead and cut the top. We'll scoop the seeds out first."

Very carefully, Jenny moved the knife into the hard pumpkin shell where it promptly stuck.

"Here." Zach leaned around Jenny. He wrapped his right hand around the knife. "I don't think this is the best knife for carving," he whispered against her cheek. "But let's go with it. Maybe it will work with the strength of the two of us." Zach pressed the knife into the pumpkin shell. Slowly, he carved a circle in the top of the pumpkin. As he worked, Zach inhaled the soft scent of lavender in Jenny's hair.

Jenny shifted in his arms, and looked up at him. A bit of pumpkin seed landed on her cheek and Zach moved his finger along the edges of her face. He removed the pumpkin seed and gazed into her warm eyes. He gently caressed the edges of her face until he reached her lips. Slowly, he traced the softness of her lips as they parted.

****

Jenny tilted her head upward and closed her eyes. Zach's gentle touch made her insides melt. She knew it was wrong—they were friends and she never wanted to lose that friendship—yet, she didn't want to stop him. Everything about Zach felt so right.

Everything.

Zach's lips touched hers. "Jenny," Zach whispered against her mouth.

"Yes." She pressed closer to Zach, and waited for that moment when his lips met hers. The moment she dreamed about for years.

118

And then the porch's screen door opened. "It's getting dark. People should be arriving..." Sadie stopped.

Flustered, Jenny broke apart from Zach. She licked her lips and ran her hand through her hair. She couldn't look up at Sadie. What would Sadie think about her kissing Zach?

"Mmm," Sadie said. "Maybe Caitlin is right. Maybe it is a magical pumpkin."

Zach cleared his throat and leaned back on his hands. He stretched his legs out in front of him. "We had a hard time with the carving knife. Is there a better one in the kitchen we could use?"

"I'm sure Hailey can find one," Sadie said. "She's knee deep in those caramel apples with Caitlin. I think Caitlin eats them just as fast as Hailey makes them."

"I'll help you look for a knife." Jenny jumped up and brushed imaginary dirt off her jeans. She felt relieved to have a reason to escape from Zach. Her emotions crashed inside her. She almost kissed Zach. What would happen to their friendship? A brisk, breeze blew across the yard and scattered the leaves, but it felt extremely hot on the porch. Jenny wiped her hand across her forehead.

"Well," Zach said. "I guess I better get over to the barn and see if Damon and Patrick need any help with the setup." Zach stood and took a step off the porch. He turned and called out to Jenny, "See you in a few minutes in the barn? The coffin waits."

Jenny grinned. For a minute, she forgot her conflicted emotions about Zach. She looked forward to her role at the haunted barn. The coffin was an old box used in a magic show. She picked it up at an estate sale. Jenny thought the coffin would look nice in the store window for a Halloween display. However, store owner, Amy disagreed. Amy insisted the front window showcase items people wanted on their Thanksgiving table, and not Halloween. Disappointed, Jenny enlisted Zach's help. Together, the two of them hauled the box to the storage shed where Jenny kept for her other sale finds. She hoped one day all her treasures would find good homes. As soon as she and Hailey came up with the idea of a haunted barn at the Elmheart Hotel, Jenny knew the box would be perfect for a coffin. She enlisted Zach's help to take the box over to the barn. During the trip, they joked about who would get to lie inside the coffin.

Jenny spent a couple days, at the barn, painting the box a night sky black. She decorated it with white, artificial cobweb strands. Jenny planned to lie on a flat board dressed like a mummy. As people walked by, she would sit up and let out an earth-shattering shriek. Jenny practiced her shriek as she drove. The only thing she insisted was the coffin must be kept open the whole time. Jenny didn't mind acting the part, but she didn't want to become trapped inside. Everyone agreed with her request.

Patrick volunteered to give the guided tours and make sure every visitor made it out the other side of the barn. Damon would be in charge of the ghoulish sound effects. Zach wanted to stand guard at the front and collect the ticket money. On the porch, Sadie would tell fortunes and in the front yard, Hailey planned to help with the apple bobbing and hand out Halloween treats with Caitlin. Jenny had been looking forward to Halloween for weeks. She wouldn't ruin it with her silly emotions about Zach.

"See you in a few," Jenny said to Zach. Her heart crashed against her throat as she looked into his warm brown eyes, but she held firm and strong in his gaze.

"I'll count on it," Zach said. He grinned and jumped off the porch like a teenage boy instead of a thirty-year-old man.

"Someone got Zach in a good mood," Sadie said slyly.

Jenny turned and faced Sadie. Heat rose to her face as she tried not to look Sadie in the eyes. "We're just friends."

"That kiss didn't look like friends to me," Sadie said. "If I didn't know better, I would say my brother is very much in love with you. I don't know when I last saw him so happy."

"That's not possible." Jenny shook her head vigorously. "We can't be anything more than friends. I don't want to lose his friendship or yours."

"Who says you have to lose anyone's friendship?" Sadie asked. "I think you and Zach would be wonderful. We've waited a long time for him to find the right girl."

"Who says that girl is me?" Jenny asked. Her voice shook.

"Oh, Jenny." Sadie stepped forward and put her arm around Jenny's shoulder. "I've seen it in your eyes for a long time. I've seen how you look at him. It's okay to be in love with Zach. From what I just saw on the porch, I think he likes you very much too."

"I don't know," Jenny said softly. "What if things don't work out? It seems so much easier to just be friends."

"Matters of the heart are never easy," Sadie said lightly. "But they're worth it, trust me. Just trust your heart. It'll tell you."

A loud crash inside the Elmheart Hotel caused them to whirl around. Sadie opened the screen door. "Hailey? Caitlin? Is everything okay?"

"Mom just dropped the tray of caramel apples," Caitlin said as she danced out of the kitchen, her eyes wide and long strands of caramel hanging from her chin.

"Oh my," Sadie said. "I think you better find something else to do for a little while. Why don't you go out to the porch and see if you can help carve the pumpkin?"

"Jenny and Zach are supposed to carve it." Caitlin stuck her hands on her hips. "Why aren't they carving the pumpkin?"

"Jenny and Zach have other things to do," Sadie said, firmly. "I think the pumpkin is your job now."

Jenny swallowed her smile. Sadie would be a great mom to the twins.

"Can I have another caramel apple?" Caitlin pleaded.

"You'll have to ask your mom," Sadie said. "Now go carve that pumpkin."

Caitlin twirled around on her heel and opened the front door.

"Well," Sadie said and wiped her forehead. "I hope my own children aren't so challenging."

"I'm sure they will be," Jenny said and smiled. "But, I'm sure you and Damon will be great with them."

There was another loud crash from the kitchen. Jenny whirled around, but before she could go see what happened, Sadie put her arm on Jenny's. "Go on out to the barn. We can take care of this."

"Sadie…" Jenny said and stopped.

"Don't worry," Sadie put her finger to her lips. "Your secret is safe with me," she said and smiled, "for now."

Jenny hugged Sadie and hurried out the side door of the hotel. Maybe Sadie was right. What if she did trust her heart? Things didn't always turn out bad. Look at Sadie and Damon or Patrick and Hailey. They all found their true love. What if Zach was her true love? Jenny's heart danced as she wound her way through the small tombstones lying along the front yard. She and Zach found the gray stones at a garage sale that summer. The tombstones were perfect for the Elmheart's front yard. She and Zach loaded the tombstones into the back of his truck and then climbed into the front. They received quite a few comments when they stopped for ice cream at the pier. A couple kids wanted to climb in the truck and check out the tombstones. Zach allowed the kids to ask questions and explore everything. Even when one of the older teens looked like he could whip out a knife at any moment, Zach simply greeted him by name and talked to the boy about his summer school work and if he was keeping up with everything. Zach's patience and kindness with the street kids were things Jenny loved. Her insides warmed. There were a lot of things she loved about Zach.

The sound of hammers and a saw greeted Jenny as she pushed open the back doors of the barn. The former animal stalls were divided into rooms with a scary scene in each stall. A small roped path guided people through the barn. Heavy, white, fake cobwebs hung everywhere.

At the doorway, Jenny leaned over and picked up a half-empty can of black paint. She walked to the back of the barn where cans of paint lined the shelves. There were paint cans for all the rooms she had painted this summer. Jenny read through the list: cream, pastel green and light blue. Every color reflected the sparkling lake water outside the windows of the hotel.

"Jenny!" Damon called from the left side of the barn. "Your coffin is over here."

Jenny smiled as she stepped toward Damon. The haunted barn promised to be a great night for everyone.

"I've got the music cued," Damon said. "But if something goes wrong, you can always just sit up and scream. I don't think anyone will know the difference."

"It looks great." Jenny reached inside and pulled out the mummy costume. "Can you help me with this?"

"I got it," Zach said as he stepped up beside her. The mummy outfit was a large, white suit with fake bandages attached to it. There was a scarf to wear over her head, leaving only her eyes showing. Jenny insisted she could use gauze tape as a wrap, but when Sadie was looking for her fortune teller costume, the shop owner gave her a deal—two costumes for the price of one.

"Step in," Zach said, his eyes twinkling at her.

Carefully, Jenny placed one hand on Zach's shoulder to balance herself. Lifting one foot then the other, she stepped into the costume. Once she was firmly inside the outfit, Jenny leaned down and grasped hold of the sides to pull it up so the mummy suit fit around her.

"Whoooo…" Patrick said. "That is a mummy!"

"Do I look okay?" Jenny asked.

"Here," Zach said gruffly behind her. "Let me zip you up."

Jenny stood still as Zach pulled up the zipper. His hands rested on her shoulders as he stood behind her. She could feel his warm breath on the back of her neck as he moved the zipper up her back. Jenny shivered.

Once she was inside and tightly zipped up, Zach handed her the scarf to wear over her head. "It looks kind of hot in there. You could wait to slip it on."

"I'm okay," Jenny said. Inside, she felt warmth creep through her body. Zach's concern touched her.

"I'll cue the music." Patrick told her. "I've got it set on the playlist for the whole barn. It'll come around to the Mummy's Walk every fifth song. At that point, you should have a group of people all waiting to be scared standing on the pathway in front of the coffin. You'll sit up and give your scary scream and then lie back down."

"Sounds easy," Jenny said. "But I think I might need a little help walking in this thing. She took a step and lurched backward as Zach's arms wrapped firmly around her.

"I've got you," he said, huskily. "Take my hand and lean on me. I'll escort you to the coffin."

Jenny slipped her hand into Zach's and his warm fingers wrapped around hers. He squeezed her hand and smiled at her. "You'll be great."

"Thanks." Jenny returned the lighthearted hand squeeze. Her heart pounded with anticipation.

Slowly, Zach escorted her to the edges of the coffin. "Your box is waiting, Mummy."

Jenny stared into the coffin. Suddenly, with great horror, she realized she would not be able to get inside. The mummy suit made it impossible for her to move her legs. "I can't..." Jenny stopped.

"Hold on," Zach said and with a great swoop, he lifted Jenny into his arms and placed her carefully into the box.

She sat up and grinned. "I'm not sure I can lie down in here and sit back up again."

"How about if you sit like that?" Zach asked. "When the people walk by, pretend you are dead. Then, as the music cues, open your mouth and let out that scream."

"Like this?" Jenny opened her mouth and released the scream she practiced for weeks.

Zach rubbed his ears. "I think you've got it."

"Zach…" Jenny said. She gazed directly into his eyes. This was the moment. She was going to tell him how she felt. Sadie was right. She would trust her heart and it would all work out.

"Jenny…" Zach began, but stopped when his cell phone rang. "Sorry," he muttered, glancing at the caller ID on the screen. "I've got to take this."

Jenny swallowed the words into her throat which felt as tight as the mummy suit.

****

Zach turned himself slightly away from Jenny, but not far enough he couldn't see the hurt splash across her face. He should have just let the phone ring. He wasn't on duty. He didn't have to answer it. But, responding to calls was second nature. He couldn't turn it off.

Zach kicked a piece of hay under his left shoe as his commanding officer spoke rapidly in his ear. Officer Thomas called in sick. It was Halloween. They couldn't be short staffed tonight. They needed him. It was his duty. But, what about Jenny and the haunted barn? Zach had never felt as close to her as he did tonight. But, was that a good thing? Jenny deserved someone who could be there for her. She deserved someone who could give her a solid and stable home, not someone who was always rushing out to the streets and stepping into danger. Zach closed his eyes. It was much easier to deal with the issues on the street than with his heart.

"Zach?" Officer Briton said in his left ear.

"I'm here," Zach said. "I can come in for a few hours."

Patrick hustled by Zach muttering something under his breath about lights and music.

Zach clicked off his phone and stuck it in his pocket. "I need to go," Zach said curtly to Patrick.

"Now?" Patrick asked. "The line outside is three feet deep. We really need you."

"It'll just be for a little bit," Zach said. "I'll be back as soon as I can."

"Okay." Patrick looked around him toward Jenny in the coffin. "We can stage the coffin so no one needs to be in it. I'll ask Jenny to do crowd control in front of the barn. She can take your place."

Zach remembered all the hours Jenny worked on the coffin. He remembered how disappointed she had been when Amy didn't want to use the coffin for the display in the window. Now, the same thing was happening. Jenny's artistic work would go to waste. The coffin would sit empty. No one would know that a mummy was supposed to sit up and screech an ear curdling wail and it would be because of him. The weight on Zach's shoulders bore down on him.

"What's going on?" Jenny asked from inside the coffin.

"Zach has to go in to work," Patrick said. "We'll need someone to take the tickets at the front."

"I can do it," Jenny said. "Not a problem. Can someone help me out of this costume and up to the front of the line?"

Zach cupped his hands into a small fist. He never should have answered the phone. If he had just let the phone ring, he would be standing at the front of the line, Jenny would be in her coffin and they would be laughing about how much fun it was at the haunted barn. Instead, he walked over to Jenny and lifted her out of the coffin. He couldn't meet her eyes. Jenny's arms wound around him as he gently placed her to the ground. Feeling terrible, but not knowing how to tell her how he felt, Zach stepped behind Jenny and lowered the zipper of her costume.

As Zach followed Jenny to the front of the barn, he noticed every little thing about her—the way she moved, the way her hair bounced across her shoulders. Why had he been so foolish? He should have said he was busy tonight. He should have said he couldn't come in to work. But instead, he had done what he always did—he ran from love and his feelings.

When Zach and Jenny reached the front of the barn, a large crowd gathered outside. Streams of car were making their way into the parking lot. Would

Jenny remember to count the people going into the barn? The fire code dictated there could only be so many people in the barn at a time.

Zach pushed to the front of the barn and up to a red table. A large cash box sat beneath the table. Zach found the silver box during a garage sale hunt with Jenny. Zach remembered how he tucked the box away. On the way home, he surprised Jenny with his ability to find treasures too. Zach pulled open the table drawer and dug around inside until his hands reached the small metal counter. Tucking the gadget inside his pocket, he hurried over to Jenny.

"You'll need this." Zach pressed the counter into her hand.

Surprised, Jenny looked up at him. "Thanks. I wouldn't have thought of it."

"Years of supervising large events in small places," Zach said swiftly. He looked into Jenny's eyes and felt himself melt. The last thing he wanted to do was go out onto the streets. He wanted to be with Jenny and share the night with her.

Suddenly, Zach wanted to tell her now. He wanted to tell her everything. "Jenny, I—"

"It's show time!" Damon called as he yanked open the large barn doors with a giant whoosh.

Zach's words were swallowed by the noisy crowd of people pushing into the front entryway of the barn.

****

Jenny pushed on the small clicker in her hand. For the last ten minutes, a steady stream of people kept her busy and stopped her from thinking about Zach. She had been so close to telling him how she felt. So close and then the moment was gone. Jenny loved knowing Zach was out on the streets, protecting everyone on Halloween night. It made her feel safe. She just wished she had followed her heart and told him how she felt before he left.

Suddenly, the lights above Jenny's head gave a large whirl and shut off. Jenny blinked rapidly in the dark. Screams echoed from within the barn—screams that Jenny felt sure were from real fright. "Don't panic," she told herself. It's just a little technical failure. Everything will be okay. The important thing was not to lose sight of the money box. They'd made quite a bit of money on ticket sales. It would go a long way toward the grand opening holiday party.

Slowly, Jenny breathed in and out. Inside the barn, flashlights bobbed as Damon lead groups of people out the back door.

"It's okay, everyone," Patrick called from the rafters. "Just a little technical malfunction. We'll have everything working again soon."

Warm arms enclosed her. Jenny opened her mouth to scream when a familiar voice said, "This way." A warm hand reached out to hers. Jenny slipped her hand into the one she'd known for so long. Zach led her out of the dark barn.

"Are you okay?" Zach asked.

"What are you doing here?"

"I stopped in at the kitchen to tell Hailey I was leaving," Zach said, "By the time I reached my car, I saw the barn lights go out. I heard the shouts and I came back. I was worried about you."

"It's just a little malfunction," Jenny said. "I think Patrick and Damon have everything under control."

"No," Zach said, his voice husky and deep. "It's more than that. I saw the lights go out. I knew you were in there. If anything happened to you, I couldn't stand the thought of you not knowing how I feel."

Jenny swallowed hard.

"Jenny," Zach said. "I care about you."

"I care about you too," Jenny said, dizzy with emotions. "We've been friends for so long. How could I not care about you?"

"It's more than that," Zach said. "I care about you as more than a friend. I have for a long time. I've just been too much of a coward to tell you how I feel." Zach said in a rush of emotion. "I love you."

133

"Oh Zach," Jenny said. "I've loved you for a long time too. I wanted to tell you tonight but when you had to go to work, I thought the moment was gone forever."

"I'll quit my job," Zach said. "I'll take a desk job in the office."

"What?" Jenny stepped back from Zach. She stared hard at him. "Why would you do that?"

"It's not fair to you," Zach said. "I can't ask you to risk your heart every night I go out on the streets."

"Oh Zach," Jenny said, and quickly stepped forward to lean against his chest. "Don't you know I feel safe with you patrolling the streets? I would never ask you to leave a job you love. I want you to be out there, doing what you love. It makes me love you more."

Zach pulled Jenny close to him in an embrace. "You are amazing." Softly, he lowered his lips to Jenny's. "Thank you."

Jenny closed her eyes as Zach's lips met hers. His arms wrapped around her tight. Her whole body warmed as her world slipped into its right place with Zach.

"The fortune teller was right," Sadie said gleefully.

Jenny pulled herself away from Zach, but his arms stayed wrapped tight around her in a protective embrace. "Yes," Jenny said and smiled at Sadie. "The fortune telling was right."

Caitlin bounced up and down beside Sadie "It was the pumpkin! The magic pumpkin."

"I think the magic pumpkin might have had something to do with it," Zach said as the music in the barn and lights clicked back on.

"Show time!" Patrick called from the open barn door. "It's time for Halloween fun!"

"Happy Halloween, Jenny." Zach lowered his lips to hers.

"Happy Halloween, Zach," Jenny said against his warm lips.

Happy Halloween!

Love's Christmas Gift

"Elizabeth is under the mistletoe!" Madison leaned over the balcony. She tied a red velvet bow to the wood banister.

"Be careful, Madison." Elizabeth gazed up at her nineteen-year-old niece on the second floor balcony. She glanced past the mistletoe hanging from a small, green tack in the living room doorway. Elizabeth shook her head and smiled. It was good to have Madison home from college for the holidays. She brought liveliness to the house. Elizabeth shifted a large glass snow globe to her left hand, and reached up to pull the mistletoe down. Before her fingers touched the ribbon, Bill stepped up behind her. A large strand of holiday lights dangled from his fingertips.

"Guess that means we kiss." Bill leaned down and kissed Elizabeth on the lips with a loud smack.

"There is nothing as wonderful as Christmas kisses." Sadie entered the room carrying a plate of decorated sugar cookies on a silver tray. A Santa hat perched sideways on her head. Sadie's dark eyes danced and her smile lit up her face. An apron covered her dark purple sweater and jeans.

Bill stepped out of the doorway. He whistled an unrecognizable tune as he headed for the front porch. Elizabeth walked quickly away from the mistletoe. Her face felt hot. Santa would not deliver her long-time friend, Bill, under her Christmas tree as a romantic partner. Bill made it clear to everyone he was a confirmed bachelor who did not want to be married. And, Bill's decision suited her fine. After her first husband left to be with another woman, Elizabeth didn't want to be married again. It was much easier to be friends.

"I'll get these lights strung on the front porch." Bill pulled open the front door. "Be back in a few minutes."

"Madison," Elizabeth said. "The top two ribbons on the stairway are sideways. Can you straighten them?"

Elizabeth set the glass snow globe on the dining room sideboard. She broke off a small piece of sugar cookie from Sadie's platter and tasted it.

"I think Bill needed to cool off from the kiss." Sadie winked at her.

"Mmmm..." Elizabeth picked up the second half of the cookie and popped it in her mouth. She ignored Sadie's hint about Bill. For months, Sadie had been trying to play match- maker between her and Bill. Sadie was probably the one who supplied the mistletoe for Madison to hang. "What recipe did you use for these?" Elizabeth took another bite of cookie.

"The holiday lunch recipe," Sadie said.

"Of course!" Elizabeth loved Sadie's holiday lunch. Every Christmas, Sadie filled her Bed and Breakfast with her friends and family. The menu changed every year, but what never changed was the small plate of homemade baked goodies Sadie gave to all her friends. Sadie's mom had owned a bakery and Sadie inherited all of her recipes. Each Christmas, Sadie surprised everyone with a new recipe.

"I wrapped all the cookies in red and green plastic wrap," Sadie said. "There should be enough for every guest who comes to your house on the tour."

"I don't know what I would have done without you." Elizabeth's eyes watered. Her friends had been amazing. Over the last couple of hours, Cassie, Sadie and Bill transformed her house into a beautiful home filled with wonderful Christmas scents and decorations. Sadie worked hard in the kitchen creating delicious Christmas goodies. Cassie made sure wreaths and garlands hung from every room in the house, and Bill had been busy hanging lights on the front porch.

"Stepping up at the last minute and offering your home on the Holiday Parlor Tour was a very gracious thing to do for the Historical Society. Who would have dreamed that Mrs. Fitch's house would be flooded by a water pipe break, and Mrs. Patterson would get sick with the flu," Cassie said from her perch on the stepladder by the fireplace. She adjusted the wreath to the left so it was placed perfectly over the mantel. A row of handmade needlepoint stockings hung underneath. Elizabeth suspected the stockings were from Cassie's own Christmas decorations.

"I'm glad to do it," Elizabeth said. "I love to share my home at the holidays. I just haven't..." Elizabeth broke off as the tears filled her throat. She'd been trying so hard not to think about her sister and brother-in-law. But the holidays brought everything so much closer to the surface. Although they hadn't talked about it, Elizabeth knew the holidays had to be hard for Madison, too. Madison was a sophomore at the University of San Diego. It hadn't surprised Elizabeth when Madison was accepted into a college across the country. Elizabeth suspected Madison wanted to get far away from where her parents had been killed in the dreadful New Year's Eve accident. But, she missed having Madison closer. It was so good to have her home for the holidays.

Sadie set down the plate of cookies and hugged Elizabeth. "I know this time of year must be extremely hard for you. We are here for you if you need anything."

Elizabeth wiped her eyes. "At least Madison was able to get home from college. Last year, she got caught in a snow storm in Chicago and got stuck in the airport on Christmas Day. If it wasn't for your holiday lunch, I don't know what I would have done."

"You are always welcome at the holiday lunch," Sadie said warmly.

Suddenly, the front door swung open and crashed against the wall.

"Ho, ho, ho! Santa has a tree for you!"

Elizabeth peered around the corner and gasped. Sailing Board treasurer, Eric, and his nephew, sixteen-year-old Devon, were engulfed in the biggest Christmas tree Elizabeth had ever seen.

"Over here." Bill walked behind Eric and Devon. "Careful. Watch the doorway. Turn the tree around." Bill was as comfortable in her house directing the tree decorating as he was on the waters directing his crew.

Elizabeth smiled. It was why everyone wanted to crew with Bill, and he so rarely had any openings.

Elizabeth hurried to the living room and moved the coffee table out of the way.

"Eric! Where did you get that tree?" Cassie waved her hand in the air. Her diamond engagement ring sparkled. Cassie had made it clear to Eric she didn't want a large diamond engagement ring. She protested a huge ring would be something to worry about while she was painting and working as an artist. But, when Eric told her the ring belonged to his grandmother who was married to his grandfather for sixty-two years, Cassie immediately softened. Elizabeth hadn't seen her take the ring off.

Elizabeth looked around the room at her friends and smiled. Over the last year, love had crept over the Sailing Foundation board members. First, Sadie reconnected with high school sweetheart Damon during a sailing regatta. Then, Cassie rekindled with her first love, Eric when the two of them were tossed together in planning the Foundation's auction. Love cast a magic spell and wound its way around the Board table. A picture of dancing with Bill at a Christmas wedding filled Elizabeth with a sudden longing.

Don't go there, she chided herself. She and Bill would always be friends. Both had full lives with their careers and community activities. It was enough to be each other's companion at yearly events such as the annual dinner dance at the Sailing Club. They didn't need to be romantically involved too.

Eric hoisted the tree into a large stand in front of the picture window.

"How does it look?" Bill asked.

"Wonderful." Elizabeth clasped her hands together and applauded lightly.

"Great!" Bill smiled at her. The wrinkles around his cheeks crinkled. Elizabeth had a strong urge to step forward and run her fingers lightly over those wrinkles. Surprised at herself and her emotions, she turned away from the festivities and walked briskly into the dining room. The best way to push aside her foolish, romantic visions was to become busy. Elizabeth pulled out a plush red velvet chair at the dining room table. There was plenty to do to get ready for the Holiday Parlor Tour. She sat down in front of her laptop. A large manila folder labeled "house" lay open on the table. Each house on the Holiday Tour was required to have a House Information Sheet. The information told visitors the age of the home, the date of purchase, how many owners it had, and if there were any interesting stories about the home. Since her home had been a last minute addition, Elizabeth wouldn't be in the tour booklet. But, Historic Homes president, Marcie, promised to tuck her information into an insert pocket of the booklet.

Elizabeth quickly typed the required information and saved the file. She glanced up once, and, seeing the tree moving sideways toward her window, quickly glanced down again. There was no point in worrying. Things were under control in Bill's capable hands. Elizabeth clicked over to her email to send the information sheet to Marcie. She logged in and frowned at the top email's subject: Job Interview. She hadn't applied for any jobs.

Curious, Elizabeth opened the email.

Dear Elizabeth,

We have recently had an opportunity to see the curriculum you designed for the Rochester Zoo. We were very impressed. As you may know, The San Diego Zoo is opening a new Safari Park. We are looking for a director to head the education department. We wondered if you might be interested in interviewing. If so, we are conducting interviews the second week of January. We'd love to interview you for the job. Please contact us at your earliest convenience.

Elizabeth inhaled sharply. After Zoo funding had been cut, she lost her job as Education Director. But, a month later, the zoo needed someone to design a science curriculum. They hired Elizabeth as a freelancer. Elizabeth enjoyed the work and hoped to find more freelance work in the New Year. Budgets at zoos were tight. She never dreamed someone would offer to interview her for a full-time job. Her pulse raced. Should she take the interview?

Madison's voice carried across the room as she directed Bill to straighten the tree. Elizabeth's heart warmed. A job in San Diego would be perfect. She would be close to Madison. They'd be able to see each other more than just Christmas and summer holidays. But— Elizabeth scanned the festive room—how could she leave? Her friends and her life were here. After her first marriage ended so disastrously, she'd taken over her parents' home. They wanted to move to Florida and retire. Elizabeth longed for the familiarity of the house where she grew up. Gradually, over the years, she updated the house. She replaced old, worn out carpet and put down new floors. She updated the kitchen to include sparkling silver appliances. She even created a sweeping attic room on the third floor for Madison.

"Aunt Elizabeth?" Madison said. "Is everything okay?"

Elizabeth shook herself. "Yes, everything is fine. I opened my email to send a note to Marcie. I started reading other emails. It's nothing." Elizabeth laughed nervously.

Madison stared hard at her.

"Really," Elizabeth said. "I'm fine. Why don't you see if you can find the box of ornaments in my bedroom closet?"

Madison frowned but didn't argue. She headed down the hall toward Elizabeth's bedroom.

Elizabeth turned back to the computer. She attached her House Information Sheet to the email and typed in Marcie's name. Elizabeth hit send. Her heart pounded and her hands felt sweaty. She didn't have to decide about the interview now. She could wait until after Christmas to make her decision. Elizabeth looked out the window at the falling snow and shivered. The winter months did get long in New York. Maybe she would go to San Diego, just to interview. It couldn't hurt. Elizabeth smiled to herself. Maybe she didn't need to fall in love like the rest of her friends. Maybe her love would be a new job.

Elizabeth stood, pushed in her chair, and looked up to meet Bill's gaze from across the room.

****

Bill hastily looked away from Elizabeth, but not before he saw the emotions cascading across her face. Bill frowned. Elizabeth wasn't known for displaying her emotions easily. In the midst of a crisis, Elizabeth could be counted on to keep her cool. Bill remembered the first time he saw Elizabeth. It was the Sailing Club Regatta three years ago. Ann had gotten sick and Elizabeth stepped up to take her place at the registration table. Midway through registration, Drew showed up with his unregistered boat of sailors. Instead of turning them away, Elizabeth calmly sorted through the registration packets until she found a handful of blank ones. She instructed Drew and his sailors to return the papers to her when they were finished. In that moment, Bill knew Elizabeth had to be on the Sailing Foundation Board. That year, he was the Board president. It seemed every time he turned around, there was another crisis. Everyone had lost their patience. More than one person threated resignation. Elizabeth rose to the challenge gracefully, and, by Christmas, the Sailing Foundation Board was back on track.

Bill scanned the warmly lit living room. The smell of cinnamon and vanilla rose from a candle on a nearby coffee table. Lamps on coffee tables spilled warm soft light onto plush carpets. Heavy red carpets covered the polished wood hallway floors and the dark oak dining table looked as though it had been in someone's family for years. Throw pillows dotted the brown leather couch and a knitted blanket lay across a matching chair. It was the home of someone who loved entertaining, and yet at the same time, the home could easily accommodate an intimate dinner for two. Bill imagined himself sitting in front of the fireplace, listening to Elizabeth talk about her day, telling her about his, and sharing long, intimate snowy evenings together.

Startled, Bill shook himself. Elizabeth was a friend. She was a good friend and a wonderful companion. It was best to leave things just as they were. When the edges started getting pushed, things got messy. He didn't like messy entanglements. They reminded him too much of his life as a boy. It was easier to live a simple life—unattached.

Bill turned his attention to the living room where Sailing Board treasurer, Eric and his nephew, Devon, tried to position a tree in front of the picture window.

"Devon," Bill said firmly. "The tree needs to lean a little to the left. It's not straight."

"This way?" Devon pushed against the tree. The branches touched the living room window.

"Not that way," Eric snapped. "The other way."

"Patience," Bill said mildly. "He's doing fine."

"I should have left him at home." Eric grumbled. "I don't seem to have any patience with him. Cassie is doing her best in the Art mentor program, but I'm not seeing much improvement at home."

"He'll get the hang of it," Bill said. "Holidays can be a rough time for people. Devon's getting used to living with you. He'll work things out." Bill watched Devon straighten the tree. "That's it." Bill gave Devon the thumbs up signal. "You got it." Bill liked Devon. He was reminded of himself at sixteen. Devon was a teen struggling to find his way in a world that had been less than kind. Devon's mom had been in and out of jail for drugs most of his life. She'd recently been sentenced to a fifteen-year sentence, and Devon had come to live with Eric. Devon didn't know his dad. Bill knew that a boy needed his dad—especially at sixteen. Cassie was working with Devon in the Art Mentor Program, which was part of the court ordered program Devon participated in after he got caught tagging graffiti. Although Eric claimed he hadn't seen any changes, Bill noticed differences. Devon spent time working at the boatyard after school. Devon was changing from a sullen young man into a young man with curiosities and a thirst for learning. Bill had already promised Devon a spot crewing on his boat next season. Devon was eagerly devouring maps and charts. Bill knew Devon would make a great long-haul racer.

Cassie stepped down from the ladder where she had been hanging a large wreath. She snuggled up against Eric. "It's snowing hard. I've got to get to the art supply store."

"I've got the truck," Eric said. "If you're ready, we can go now."

Sadie came in from the kitchen. She wiped her hands on her apron. "I better go too. I've got a house full of guests at the bed and breakfast."

"I'll come with you." Madison hopped down from the stairs. "You'll need an extra set of hands setting up the breakfast dishes for the morning."

"But, what if the snow continues, Madison?" Elizabeth pushed back her chair at the dining room table. "I won't be able to get the car out of the driveway to pick you up. They always plough the street and push the piles of snow onto the bottom of the driveway."

"I'll stay and help with the tree." Bill leaned against the doorway of the living room. Suddenly, the last thing he wanted to do was leave. He never decorated for Christmas and it would be cold and dark in his one bedroom apartment. He wanted to spend the rest of the cozy afternoon in the house with Elizabeth.

"Oh, no," Elizabeth protested. "I don't want you to have to stay. The tree only needs a few lights and ornaments. I'm perfectly capable of doing that myself."

"It's always easier to hang lights with two people," Bill said, and smiled at Elizabeth. "Plus, I'm pretty good with a shovel."

"Thank you," Elizabeth said. Pink darkened her cheeks. "Thank you for helping with everything." She waved her hand toward the living room. "The house looks wonderful."

With a start, Bill realized Elizabeth was not used to accepting help from her friends. She was the one who usually pitched in to help everyone else. This time, everyone else was helping Elizabeth.

In the hallway, there was a quick flurry of jackets, coats, and boots being slipped on and everyone headed out the door in one large group. Once the door shut, the house seemed very quiet.

"Well," Bill stuck his hands in his pockets and shifted on his feet. He and Elizabeth had often been each other's companions to many events, but they were never alone—just the two of them. "Where do you keep the Christmas tree lights?" It was always easier to keep busy. As a boy, Bill learned the best way to not think about what was going on at home was to keep busy. At school, he played sports year-round. Once the coaches found out about his dad's constant unemployment, there was always someone willing to step up and help out with his uniform fees. He thrived at sports. They gave him a place to be in the afternoons and evenings. It didn't bother him that he never had anyone attend his games. He was just happy to have somewhere to go.

"In the spare bedroom closet." Elizabeth turned and walked down the hall. Her heels clicked on the hard wood floors. Bill followed behind her. Artwork decorated the walls and when he looked closely, Cassie's name was on the bottom of three pieces. Bill grinned. Elizabeth was the anonymous bidder at the Sailing Club's silent auction.

At the end of the hall, Elizabeth pulled opened the spare bedroom door and walked across the thick, plush carpet. A colorful quilt covered the bed and thick pillows rested at the headboard. An old dresser with a handful of black and white photos sat in the corner. A small teddy bear perched in a white wicker chair on top of a red cushion. Bill wanted to lie down on the bed and take a long nap while the snow drifted past the windows.

"No naps," Elizabeth said, and smiled at him.

"Just a little one." Bill winked.

"No." Elizabeth playfully bumped him with her hip. He bumped her back.

Elizabeth laughed and opened a closet door. Inside, were stacks of plastic bins, each one neatly labeled: Christmas tree lights, Angel Christmas ornaments, Gold ball ornaments and Sailing ornaments.

"All of these?" Bill asked. He didn't know a tree needed so many ornaments.

Elizabeth studied the boxes. "We'll take the tree lights and the gold ball ornaments. I don't think we'll make this one themed, so we won't need the angel ornaments."

"Themed?"

"Sometimes I like to decorate the trees with a theme." Elizabeth pointed to a large plastic bin at the bottom of the closet. "One year, everything was in miniature ponies." She laughed lightly. "The tree was Madison's idea. We had a hard time finding ornaments."

"I had no idea Christmas tree decorating was so complex." Bill nodded toward the box labeled sailing ornaments. "Not the sailing ornaments?" He raised an eyebrow at her.

"Of course!" Elizabeth flushed. "The sailing ornaments. I always use the sailing ornaments."

Bill lifted a box, and finding it surprisingly light, leaned down and scooped up a second box. Bill placed the second on top of the first. Slowly, he backed out of the room. The boxes wobbled but didn't fall over.

Carefully, Bill headed down the hall to the living room. When he reached the tree, Bill opened the first box of Christmas lights. He swallowed hard as the memories flooded through him. The last time he helped with tree lights, he was fifteen. Earlier in the day, Dad cut down the tree. It was the first year Bill's older brother, Mike, didn't come home for the holidays. Mike was a police officer in California and took extra shifts over the holiday. Mike explained he and his new wife,

Bethany, needed the money. They had just bought a house and the costs were eating them alive. Bill suspected it had more to do with not wanting to spend another holiday with Dad.

The tree cutting had gone well. Dad seemed in a relative good mood, and Bill held his breath that mood would last for the rest of the day. But, by the time evening rolled around, Dad had been drinking all afternoon. Mom wanted to straighten the tree lights and Dad shoved her out of the way. Bill was furious. He couldn't stand by and do nothing. At fifteen, he had reached his full height and towered over Dad by two inches. Bill pushed Dad away from Mom. The tree hadn't been placed steady in the stand. It didn't take much for Dad to go sprawling into the Christmas tree. It tottered and crashed over.

"That's it!" Dad roared. He picked up the phone and dialed 911. The police arrived and Dad convinced them Bill assaulted them. Mom hadn't said a word and Bill was hauled off to juvenile detention. He spent the holiday sitting around a table, wearing an orange jumpsuit and watching movies. After that, Bill swore off Christmas festivities.

The one exception was the annual Sailing Foundation New Year's Dinner Dance. As a long-time member of the Board, Bill was expected to attend. When Elizabeth joined the Board, Bill immediately noticed she didn't have a companion either. Bill casually asked her if she would like to go with him. It'd been the beginning of a long friendship.

"Bill?" Elizabeth gently touched his shoulder. "Is everything all right?"

"Sure." Bill shook himself out of the memories of the past. He picked up a long strand of lights. "If you stand on one side of the tree, and I stand on the other, we can get these lights hung."

Elizabeth slipped around the back of the tree. She wrapped her arms around the tree trunk and wiggled her fingers. Bill chuckled. It looked like the tree had moving arms. Bill placed a strand of lights in her hands. His fingers touched hers, and for a minute, he felt a jolt. Bill shook his head. He was just tired and hungry. He hadn't eaten lunch and it was almost time for dinner. Unplugged tree lights didn't give his fingers jolts of electricity.

Bill waited as Elizabeth carefully threaded the lights through the branches on her side of the tree and passed them back to him Gradually, he worked them up into the branches above him and passed them back to her. Each time, his fingers touched hers, a small jolt shot through his fingertips. Maybe he needed to see a doctor. He hoped there wasn't something wrong with the nerves in his fingertips.

When the lights were completely woven among the tree branches, Elizabeth stepped from behind the tree. She flicked on a switch at the front base of the tree. The tree twinkled and sparkled.

"I never knew a tree could look so beautiful," Bill said, looking at Elizabeth's glowing face in the tree light.

"It is magic, isn't it?" Elizabeth said softly. She looked up at Bill. In her eyes, the magic spark of Christmas twinkled.

Neither of them said a word.

The grandfather clock chimed five o'clock. Elizabeth jumped. "Where has the afternoon gone?" She picked up an ornament and carefully unwrapped tissue paper. Elizabeth let out a small gasp and covered her mouth with her hand.

"What's wrong?" Bill immediately stepped to her side. He wanted to wrap his arms around her and protect her from whatever pain was inside the tissue.

"These were my sister's ornaments." Elizabeth held a gold giraffe in her hand. "I didn't mean to grab this box. This must have been the one Madison brought out earlier." Elizabeth sunk down into the plush arm chair. She placed the giraffe on the coffee table and stared at it.

"Do you want me to get a different box of ornaments?" Bill asked.

"No," Elizabeth said quietly. "I think these belong on the tree. Madison wanted them here."

Bill leaned against the chair. His thigh brushed against Elizabeth's arm. "We didn't keep our family ornaments. I don't know what happened to them." Bill studied the carpet and rubbed his left foot against the floor. "I left at sixteen. I didn't get along with my dad. I decided it'd be better on my own."

Elizabeth reached out and touched Bill's hand.

He linked his fingers with hers. "We always thought once Dad was gone, Mom would be happy to be on her own. She had his life insurance policy. My brother and I thought she'd go somewhere like Arizona or Florida. But, she never had a chance. The doctors diagnosed her with a fast growing cancer a month after Dad passed. She died six weeks later."

"I'm sorry." Elizabeth squeezed Bill's hand tightly.

"I try not to think too much about it," Bill said. "But, the holidays...." He broke off.

"It's why you understand Devon," Elizabeth said. "And all the other young people who have sailed with you over the years."

Bill shrugged. "No use sitting around crying for what is gone and not coming back."

Elizabeth leaned over and picked up the giraffe ornament. She dangled it from her fingertips. The giraffe sparkled in the red and green Christmas tree lights. "Could you help me hang this?" She pointed to the top branch. "I think it should go in the front, near the top where everyone will see it."

Gently, Bill released Elizabeth's hand. He took the ornament and placed it on the Christmas tree.

****

In the brightly lit kitchen, Elizabeth poured hot water into two large mugs. Each mug had a picture of a sailboat on it. Last fall, the Foundation designed the mugs for a fund-raiser. They took pictures of each member's boat and had them printed onto the coffee mugs. The fund-raiser hadn't been as successful as some of their others, but Elizabeth remembered having a good time with Bill. He'd been the one in charge of taking the pictures. Afterwards, they ate at the Marina Harbor Side Restaurant. She teased him because he always ordered the same thing: a burger with fries. He gave her a hard time because she couldn't make up her mind and asked the waitress a lot of questions about the menu.

Elizabeth spooned heaping scoops of cocoa into each mug and stirred. She'd been surprised to hear about Bill's family as a child. Bill didn't talk much about his past. She knew he had a brother on the West Coast, maybe Seattle, and two nephews who he sent Christmas and birthday presents to every year. But as far as she knew, Bill never went to see his brother or nephews and they never came to see him.

"Are there marshmallows in here somewhere?" Bill dug around in her pantry. His back end stuck out as he buried himself inside the shelves. Elizabeth giggled. She felt like a teenager in the kitchen with Bill.

"Top shelf, in the back," Elizabeth said.

"Got them!" Bill emerged with a packet of large marshmallows. He grinned and his eyes sparkled. "Hot cocoa is not complete without marshmallows." Bill leaned over Elizabeth's shoulder. He dropped one marshmallow into each cup. Droplets of cocoa splashed onto the counter.

Elizabeth lifted a cup and handed it to Bill. She hoisted the second cup in the air. "Cheers. We finished the tree!"

"Cheers!" Bill clinked his mug to hers and took a long sip. When he raised his head, white marshmallow foam covered his upper lip like a mustache.

Placing her cocoa on the counter, Elizabeth leaned over and wiped the foam with her second finger.

Bill reached up and took her hand. Lowering it to his lips, he gently kissed each finger.

Elizabeth couldn't move. Butterflies raced through her stomach. She felt like a child on Christmas morning.

Bill turned her hand face up and kissed her inner palm.

Elizabeth stepped closer to him. She could feel the heat radiating from Bill's body. His left arm moved around her and pulled her close to him. She tilted her face upward. He leaned down, and gently, placed his lips on hers. Parting her lips, Elizabeth opened to Bill. Unlike the mistletoe kiss, this kiss surrounded her and engulfed her. She felt herself surrendering to him just as the phone rang.

Bill broke away from her. "I'm sorry," he mumbled. "I didn't mean to…"

Elizabeth licked her lips and adjusted her slacks. She couldn't look at him. He didn't need to apologize. She enjoyed the kiss. People didn't apologize when they enjoyed something. Elizabeth ran her hands through her hair. She reached over to answer the phone and paused at the caller ID. The San Diego Zoo. It would still be mid-afternoon on the West Coast. Someone was calling to make sure she responded to the interview request. Elizabeth placed her hand on the receiver. She did not pick it up.

"Elizabeth?" Bill asked.

The phone rang two more times and then was silent. Thankfully, the answering machine was inside the phone and the person leaving a message could not be heard in the kitchen.

"It's nothing." Elizabeth licked her lips. She stepped to the window and pulled aside the blinds. "I think the snow has stopped." She peered onto the lawn. Even though it was dark, the snow made it seem very light. Elizabeth had a sudden desire to be outside. She wanted to lie down and make snow angels the way she once had as a child with her sister. She swallowed hard. If Michelle was alive, Elizabeth would have called her. She would have asked what to do about Bill. She would have told her about the kiss. She would have told her about the job interview and how she was conflicted about her feelings for Bill and her desire to have the interview. Michelle had been younger than Elizabeth by eleven months. They shared everything—clothing, toys, books, and once even a boy who had the bad luck to find himself the object of interest for both of them at the same time. It was the only time she remembered fighting with Michelle. They spent three days not speaking to each other before their mother called the boy's mother and said neither of her daughters were mature enough to date anyone.

Bill cleared his throat. "I'm going to check the porch lights. I want to make sure all the lights work."

"I'll come with you. I want to clear the snow from the bird feeder. The birds will be looking for food." Elizabeth reached under the sink. She pulled out a bag of birdseed. In the winter, she always made sure the birds had enough to eat—especially after a fresh snow when it would be hard to find food on the covered ground. Elizabeth took a deep breath and exhaled. She felt as though the house was closing in on her and she couldn't breathe. After Michelle died, her grief counselor recommended she take a series of beginner yoga classes to help with the stress of losing someone. Elizabeth didn't remember much from the classes, but she did remember there was something about breathing. Inhale. Exhale. Inhale. Exhale. Yoga breathing didn't seem to be working. Elizabeth felt her pulse racing. She just needed to get outside in the fresh air.

Holding the birdseed bag to her chest, Elizabeth walked quickly to the front door. She didn't look to see if Bill was following her. At the entryway, she snatched her down jacket from the hook. The hook hung above a small bench, and, hastily, she sat down on the bench and placed the birdseed beside her. She slipped into her boots. Elizabeth didn't bother to zip them all the way up. She would only be outside a few minutes. The snow wasn't so deep she had to worry about snow creeping over the tops. Elizabeth reached into her pocket and pulled out a hat with large, colorful pom-poms. She loved her hat. Madison made it for her when she was in middle school. Madison had a matching hat and the two of them wore them whenever they walked around the neighborhood. Madison. Elizabeth made a mental note to call Sadie when she got back inside. There was no reason for Madison to spend the night at Sadie's Bed and Breakfast. It was nice of her friends and niece to try and give her space with Bill, but she didn't need it. She would not take the chance on loving someone to have him leave, or, she thought, for her to leave him.

Elizabeth picked up the bag of birdseed, stood, and walked to the door

Behind her, Bill tapped on her shoulder.

Elizabeth whirled around. Her eyes met his and she struggled to keep her feelings under control.

Bill reached up and straightened her hat. "That's better."

"Thank you," Elizabeth said, and smiled up at him. Her heart pounded. It was so comfortable to be with Bill. It would be so easy to keep the relationship as friends. And yet, her feelings told her he meant so much more than just a friend. But, she did not want to take that risk. She couldn't take the chance.

"After you," Bill said as he pulled open the front door.

Elizabeth stepped out onto the porch. She breathed in the crisp, fresh air. Pine needles from the tree littered the front porch. But, she barely noticed. Instead, she scanned the winter wonderland in front of her. Everything always looked so fresh and new after the snow. It looked like a clean slate to write a new story on. Elizabeth breathed slowly.

Bill flicked a switch by the door and white lights twinkled across her front porch. "I would miss this…" she said.

"Miss this?" Bill turned to her.

Elizabeth gasped. She hadn't meant to speak out loud.

"Elizabeth?" Bill asked.

"It's nothing." Elizabeth shook her head.

"It was something in your email and the phone call." Bill pressed.

"I've been asked to interview for a job," Elizabeth said softly. "It's in San Diego."

"San Diego?" Bill's voice sounded far away and small.

"I'd be close to Madison," Elizabeth touched the pom-pom on her head. "But, I'd hate to leave here. I've always lived in Rochester. This was the house where I grew up. I don't know how it would be to start over so far away." She stared into the backyard. "It's just an interview. I haven't even agreed to go on it yet. I don't know…"

"I think you should do it," Bill said firmly. He reached down, picked up Elizabeth's mittened hand and squeezed. "You deserve this, Elizabeth."

Elizabeth stared into the snow-covered yard. Her heart was breaking but Bill was right. As soon as Bill left, she would go inside and send the email agreeing to an interview. Afterwards, she could spend a few weeks in San Diego. She'd visit museums, take walks on the beach, and forget about her crazy Christmas feelings about Bill.

"Yes," Elizabeth said to Bill. "I think I will do the interview. Thank you." She touched his hand briefly and headed toward the bird feeder. Her heart crashing into pieces, Elizabeth did not turn to look behind her.

***

Bill's stomach tightened. He was happy to hear about the interview and possible job opportunity. Elizabeth was extremely talented. The zoo would be foolish not to offer her the job. Bill grimaced. But, it took all his strength not to act on his feelings. There was a magnetic force that pulled him to her. He'd always thought of that feeling as friendship. But after the kiss in the kitchen, he knew it was so much more. But, he couldn't give her more. He couldn't give her marriage. He didn't have the first clue how to have a successful marriage. And he would not inflict his inability to be in a marriage on her. She deserved someone who could marry her.

Bill adjusted a strand of lights on the balcony. "Everything is set." Bill said to Elizabeth's back. "If you don't need anything else, I think I'll get going."

"Thank you." Elizabeth turned and looked up from the bird feeder. In the dark, it was impossible to see her expression.

Bill stepped off the porch and headed to his truck. He tried to steady his walk and not betray his emotions. When he reached the truck, he used his arm to wipe the snow off the front windshield. The snow crashed to the ground in one big thump.

Ten minutes later, Bill pulled into the marina. The parking lot was empty. On the docks, Bill could see a light on in his boat. Bill frowned. He didn't remember leaving a light on. Quickly, he hopped out of his car and hurried down the snow-covered dock to his boat. Rock music played softly from inside.

"Hello?"

Devon popped up from the bow of the boat. "I'm sorry to be on your boat without asking," Devon said. "I just needed somewhere…"

Bill lowered himself down the ladder and into the boat. Devon wasn't the first teen to show up on his boat unexpectedly. Bill kept a spare key hidden under the mast. Anyone who spent time with him working on the boat knew about the key. Bill didn't mind. As long as nothing was damaged and everything was replaced as it was found. Bill surveyed the boat. A sleeping bag lay across the lower bench. A small kettle steamed and the radio played softly. Devon was planning for more than a one- hour stay on the boat. "Holidays are hard, huh?" Bill asked.

Devon sat down on his unrolled sleeping bag. He fiddled with the zipper. "Yeah," he said without looking at Bill. "Everyone seems so happy. Eric has Cassie and all he can talk about is the wedding. Sadie and Damon are so happy together, I don't think I fit in so well."

Bill picked up the tea kettle. He poured the last of the hot water into a mug and dunked in a tea bag. "Why don't you grab the map?"

Devon turned around and grabbed a rolled up map from the shelf above the lower bunk bench. "How come you aren't married?" Devon asked suddenly. "I bet you'd be great with your own kids." Devon ducked his head shyly. "I'd like you as a dad."

Bill swallowed hard. "Thanks," he said gruffly. He picked up his mug and took a long drink of tea. "I guess I'm just a little nervous about the whole marriage thing. My parents didn't have a very good one. I'm not sure I'd make a very good husband."

"I bet you'd be great," Devon said. "I didn't think Eric would ever get married and look at him and Cassie."

169

"Yes," Bill said slowly. "You're right." Eric had been determined to keep to himself. He had a lot of responsibilities and he didn't feel he should involve someone else in his problems. But, when Cassie came along, Eric surrendered. Was it the same thing with Elizabeth? Could it work with her?

"You can do it," Devon said.

Bill eyed Devon over his cup. He smiled. Devon sounded like he did when he was coaching sailors how to take a boat through rocky waters. "Maybe," he said. "Maybe I could."

"What are we doing with the maps?" Devon waved his hand over the set of maps spread across the table.

"The best thing I know for taking care of the blues is planning where I'd like to sail. It helps me figure out how to chart my course. Life is a lot like sailing. Sometimes it's calm and other times storms come up. You have to know how to sail in both. But, most important, you have to know where you are headed."

"Does it work?" Devon asked.

"I've planned a lot of sailing trips this way. So yeah, I guess it does." Over the years, he'd sailed to a lot of the places he once dreamed about. He'd rented boats in the Caribbean. He sailed the Great Lakes. He sailed on the Atlantic. All the trips started with a dream and mapping the route.

"Where would you go?" Devon drew his finger down the map's waterways.

Bill perched on the bench across from Devon. "I think I might go to San Diego," he said slowly.

"San Diego!" Devon said. "That's a big sail."

Bill chuckled. "It's a big trip to plan. But," he looked at Devon's unrolled sleeping bag, "looks as though you planned to be here awhile."

Devon flushed. "Is it okay to spend the night?"

"Did you tell Eric?"

Devon looked down. He shook his head no.

"Give Eric a call," Bill said. "I'm sure you have your cell phone."

Devon reached into his pocket and pulled out the small phone. He grinned sheepishly.

"Good," Bill said. "Make a call."

Bill reached behind him and pulled down more charts. What would be the best route to San Diego?

****

On Christmas morning, Elizabeth rang the doorbell at Sadie's Bed and Breakfast. The circular driveway was packed and cars lined the street. Sadie must have invited everyone she knew this year. Elizabeth checked her wristwatch. She was running a little late for the holiday brunch and hoped everyone wasn't already eating. She'd sent Madison ahead of her and sent an email to the San Diego Zoo telling them she would be pleased to interview in January. Afterwards, Elizabeth drove over to Marcie's house to drop off a poinsettia plant. She wanted to thank Marcie for the fantastic job with the Holiday Homes Parlor Tour. Everything had gone off without a hitch and more than a couple people marveled at the beautifully decorated tree.

A large wreath hung on Sadie's front door. Elizabeth could hear the sound of music and people talking inside. She shifted a large shopping bag full of presents from her right to her left hand. Every year, Cassie, Elizabeth and Sadie promised each other no presents, and every year, there were presents. Elizabeth reached forward to ring the doorbell and then, laughing, she shook her head. It was foolish to think anyone would hear the doorbell. She placed her hand on the door knob, when, suddenly the door swung opened.

"Merry Christmas!" Bill said.

"Bill?" Bill never came to Sadie's holiday brunch. What was he doing here this year? What changed his mind?

Bill moved aside. "Come in. It's freezing out there. Let me take that." Bill reached down and lifted Elizabeth's large shopping bag out of her hand.

Elizabeth stepped into the front hallway. She slipped out of her coat and Bill stepped behind her to help her. "Thank you," Elizabeth said.

"I'll just put this in the coat room." Bill winked at Elizabeth. "It's pretty packed, but I think we can find room."

"Elizabeth!" Sadie cried. She rushed over to the front door. She wore a red velvet top with a scoop neck and a long black skirt swirled to her feet. At her throat sparkled a gold necklace in the shape of a sailboat. "I'm so glad you're here!"

"Your Christmas necklace is beautiful," Elizabeth said as Sadie enfolded her in a hug.

"Bill is here," Sadie whispered against her cheek. "Can you believe it?"

"No." Elizabeth shook her head. "Whatever changed his mind?"

Sadie drew back and looked at Elizabeth. "I think it was you."

"Me?"

"He told us you have an interview in San Diego."

"Yes," Elizabeth said. "It's just an interview. I wasn't sure if I would take it, but I decided it would be for the best. I just sent the email this morning."

Sadie winked at her. "Bill's been talking to Damon about sailing to San Diego."

"What?" Elizabeth asked.

Sadie shrugged. "He said he might want to take the boat around to San Diego. Damon is trying to convince him to take it over land and put it in the water once he gets there."

"Why would he do that?" Elizabeth said.

Sadie smiled mischievously. "Love does a lot of mysterious things."

Elizabeth looked around the crowded room for Bill. She had to talk to him. She had to tell him that he could not leave Rochester. He could not leave the teens that depended on him. He could not leave his life here.

Elizabeth spotted Bill at the food buffet. He was heaping scrambled eggs onto an already full plate. "Excuse me," Elizabeth said to Sadie. She hurried over and tapped Bill on the shoulder. "I need to talk to you."

Turning, Bill smiled at Elizabeth. "I would say the same to you." Bill set his plate down on the table.

He lowered his hand and placed it on Elizabeth's lower back. "Let's go somewhere we can talk."

"It'll be quiet in the library," Elizabeth suggested. "Sadie uses it as her office. She usually keeps the door shut during parties."

Keeping his hand on Elizabeth's lower back, Bill steered her to the library.

Elizabeth sat down on a small, leather couch and Bill sat beside her.

"Bill. You can't...."

"...go to San Diego." Bill finished.

"Yes," Elizabeth said. "Your life is all here—the teens, the Foundation, the Sailing Club. Everything."

"What if the woman I love is not?"

"The woman you love?" Elizabeth repeated slowly.

"Yes," Bill said firmly. "I don't know why I didn't see it sooner. I always thought we had a great friendship. When you told me you had a job interview in San Diego, I didn't want to stop you, but I don't want to lose you either."+

With tears in her eyes, Elizabeth looked up at Bill. "I feel the same about you. But, I don't even have a job yet. How can you make plans to take the boat?"

Bill chuckled. "Well, maybe the boat will stay here and I'll fly. But, no matter what, I can't imagine not going with you." He leaned forward and whispered against her ear, "We're going to make this work, Elizabeth."

Elizabeth reached down and threaded her fingers through Bill's. "You're the best present I have ever received on Christmas."

"I could say the same about you," Bill said. "Now, how about that mistletoe kiss?"
"There is no mistletoe hanging above us," Elizabeth said, and laughed

"Yes, there is." Bill reached into his jacket pocket and pulled out a twig of mistletoe. A small green tack was tangled in the leaves.

"You took the mistletoe when we decorated the tree!" Elizabeth exclaimed.

"Merry Christmas, Elizabeth," Bill gently placed his lips on hers.

"Merry Christmas!"

New Year
Heart Song

"It's been so much fun having you here for Christmas. Do you have to go home tomorrow?" Ten-year-old Caitlin leaned against the wood bench and unlaced her skate. A colorful, wool scarf trailed down her right side. The wind blew briskly across the frozen pond and tossed her blonde hair.

"My flight leaves the day after New Year. We still have tonight and New Year's Day." Angie tied her skates together with a neat bow. She wanted the time to slow down too. Angie picked one of Caitlin's fluffy mittens off the ground. She gave the mittens and scarf to Caitlin for Christmas.

In the days before the holiday, Angie enjoyed sitting in the thick, comfortable chairs by the roaring Elmheart Hotel fireplace. She'd knitted her niece's present and talked to her brother, Patrick, and his wife, Hailey. Angie loved sipping peppermint tea as she listened to their stories about opening the hotel. The time passed quickly and Angie finished the mittens and scarf by Christmas Eve. She wrapped them in red and gold paper and placed the gift under the Christmas tree. It made Angie happy when Caitlin selected her gift as the one she opened on Christmas Eve.

"I'll come back." Angie wrapped her scarf around her neck. The temperature had dropped significantly in the last hour of skating.

"When?" Caitlin crashed onto the bench beside Angie and pressed close against her.

"Soon." Angie gazed across the frozen skating pond. Caleb helped his seven-year-old son, Jesse, skate backwards. Both wore heavy down coats, jeans and thick gloves. Angie's stomach churned with conflicted emotions.

She met Caleb the summer between high school and college when Angie performed piano while Caleb did a vaudeville act at the amusement park's small theater. At the end of each night's performances, Angie didn't want to leave. She lingered to play her favorite songs while Caleb sat in the theater's front row. He clapped no matter how badly she missed notes. Caleb attended community college and helped his mom after a plane accident took his dad's life. He hoped to own his own theater business one day.

Angie, however, couldn't wait to leave home and go to college on the west coast. After her mom died, dad busied himself with managing his bar. He was never home and it was up to her older brother, Patrick, to help raise her. Angie wanted nothing more than a fresh start and to make a life of her own. Sometimes, Angie dreamed about marrying Caleb and having a family but it could never happen. She could never stay in their small town and make a name for herself as a pianist.

Now, ten years later, after a failed marriage and some business problems, Caleb worked as the hotel's handyman and raised Jesse as a single parent. For the last two weeks, Angie tried to push away her feelings for Caleb. She tried to pretend they were still what they had always been—friends.

"Will you come back for Valentine's Day?" Caitlin interrupted Angie's thoughts. "It's my favorite holiday."

"Valentine's Day might be a little too soon." Angie draped her right arm around Caitlin's shoulder and squeezed. "Maybe you'll come visit me. There are great beaches in Oregon."

"I don't want to visit you." Caitlin slipped out of Angie's embrace. She shuffled her heavy boots in the snow. Snow flew everywhere and added to the new, heavy, thick flakes coming down. "I want you to be here with us."

"I'm sorry." Angie's heart ached. She loved spending time with her niece. Last February, Patrick called Angie and told her he reunited with his high school sweetheart, Hailey, and discovered Caitlin was his daughter. Angie promised to return home at the holidays. She hadn't been home since her dad died over three years before.

"You could visit in the summer." Caitlin stood and twirled. Her boots left large footprints in the snow. "We have fireworks and everyone goes swimming."

My schedule is pretty booked." Angie shivered. She pulled her coat higher around her neck. She couldn't imagine swimming on the frozen pond. Angie burrowed into her turtleneck sweater. Her schedule was booked full for the next two years with recitals, performances and benefit obligations. Angie thrived on a full and busy schedule, but, lately, her schedule felt more like a burden than a joy.

"But you are here now," Caitlin said. "You must not be that busy."

Angie tightened her lips. She hadn't told anyone the reason she'd been able to fly out this holiday season. Last spring, she fought what her agent called 'the blues.' Angie tried practicing more. She tried getting more exercise. But, her lethargy affected her performances. Reviewers called her recitals lifeless and passionless. Angie's best friend, Jessica, offered the use of her home on the beach in Hawaii. Everyone said Angie needed to clear her mind. She was burned out. Angie hoped they were right. But Jessica forgot to mention the beach home was near a popular honeymoon resort. Angie returned home two days early. And to top it off, a week later, she didn't land the audition for the annual city holiday performance.

"The snow has really picked up." Caleb skated to a stop in front of Angie. He smiled down at her with a boyish grin. His dark eyes danced. "It's a good thing the guests are already at the Elmheart Hotel for New Year's Eve. It will be rough traveling tonight." Caleb pulled off his knit stocking cap. He shook his dark hair like a puppy shaking off water.

"We get stuck in the snow a lot." Jesse crashed against Caleb's leg and steadied himself. His dark hair curled down to the top of his jacket. Jet black eyes, like Caleb's, sparkled at Angie from under his hat. "Dad has old tires."

"Thanks for the vote of confidence." Caleb reached over and pulled off Jesse's hat.

Jesse giggled and yanked it out of his left hand. "Keep away!"

Caleb grabbed for the cap and missed it by a yard. "I'll get it back."

Angie's heart lifted at the joyful spirit of Caleb and his son. All afternoon, the two played more like brothers than father and son.

"The clouds are really thick over the lake." Angie moved over on the bench to make room for Jesse.

"You're not scared of a little snow?" Caleb teased. His dark eyes danced as he gazed at Angie.

"No," Angie said, and laughed. Her pulse beat faster as she looked up at Caleb. During the last two weeks, she told herself it was only the holidays that made her feel so emotional about Caleb. Everyone wanted to be in love during Christmas. But the last thing Angie needed was a romantic relationship. Her previous relationship was a disaster. Robert called her an icicle and sold the tabloids a big story. She didn't go to the grocery store for two weeks so she wouldn't have to see her face in every checkout line.

"Everyone is very excited to hear you perform tonight." Caleb took off his glove. He held out his hand to Jesse who wobbled off the ice and crashed onto the bench. Caleb knelt beside Jesse and his voice softened. "Let's get those skates off, little guy."

Angie's stomach fluttered with butterflies thinking about the New Year concert. Her Christmas gift to Patrick and Hailey was a special New Year's Eve recital in the hotel's newly refinished ballroom. Over the last two weeks, Caleb spent hours polishing the old wood floors and bringing them up to a gleaming shine. They rented a baby grand piano and placed it in the front window. The hotel's decorator, Jenny, designed vintage placemats, a table runner and a centerpiece for the large dining room table. Hailey and Patrick sold New Year's Eve hotel packages. Each guest received an overnight stay, dinner and a champagne toast at midnight.

Angie's stomach tightened. What if her performance was as lackluster as the ones she performed in Portland? In early December, the Elmheart Hotel opened and kicked off an amazing holiday season. Every room had been booked since Halloween. On Christmas Eve, Hailey served a spectacular dinner and matched it with a sumptuous Christmas Day brunch. Rooms were reserved as far in advance as the next holiday. Three summer weddings were scheduled as well as a fall fiftieth anniversary party.

The final grand opening event was the New Year's Eve dinner and dance. Community members booked every room of the hotel. The mayor and his wife reserved the Seashore Suite. Two of the city council members, and their wives, requested the Garden Suite and the adjoining room, the Daisy Room. Other guests included prominent school board members, as well as the president of a local college. Everyone expected Angie's performance to be the highlight of the season.

Jesse leaned against Angie and sniffed. His black corduroys pant legs were caked in ice and his jacket unzipped. Angie reached over to fasten Jesse's coat. "It's snowing hard," Angie said. "This will keep you warm." She slipped her hand inside her pocket and pulled out a packet of tissues. She handed one to Jesse.

"I was skating backward." Jesse wiped his nose. He crumpled the tissue and shoved it into his jacket pocket. "I want to be a professional hockey player when I grow up."

"Mmm…" Caleb muttered. He kneeled beside Jesse and unlaced his right skate. "I thought you wanted to be a veterinarian last week."

"I can be both," Jesse said.

"Of course you can." Angie loved childhood enthusiasm. She wanted to reenergize her piano playing with some of that energy.

"I can't wait for the party." Caitlin dropped to the ground and began to make an angel in the freshly fallen snow. "There will be food and dancing and champagne. Maybe I'll even find someone to kiss."

"I don't think you will have champagne." Caleb removed Jesse's skates. Jesse slipped into his boots and Caleb unlaced his own skates.

"It's New Year's Eve. Everyone drinks champagne." Caitlin rolled away from her snow angel. She picked up a handful of snow and packed it in her hand.

"I'm not sure about the kissing part either." Angie swallowed hard. She couldn't remember the last time she kissed someone on New Year's Eve. Every year, she performed in a large concert hall. At midnight, she was too busy playing Auld Lang Syne to worry about finding someone to kiss.

"Everyone kisses someone on New Year's Eve." Caitlin shuffled the snowball between her left and right hand. "Who are you going to kiss?"

Angie felt the heat creeping up her neck. "Everyone does not kiss someone at New Year's Eve. I play the piano."

"Mmmm..." Caitlin hurled the snowball. It landed at Caleb's feet with a thunk.

"Good miss." Caleb bent down and grabbed a handful of snow. He packed it and tossed the ball to Caitlin.

Beside her, Jesse pulled at Angie's left arm. "We have a surprise, don't we?"

"Yes." Angie placed her hand over his. She was grateful to talk about something besides kissing. "We do."

"I like surprises." Caleb sank down on the other side of Angie. He whispered against her cold cheek. "But, can you give me a hint? I don't like to be too surprised."

Angie inhaled Caleb's rich, deep, woodsy scent and felt the warmth of his breath. She wanted to reach out and run her hands through his curls. "No." Angie hoped her voice wasn't shaking. "If I told you, then it wouldn't be a surprise."

"Well, when do I get to see this surprise?" Caleb's voice hummed with charm.

"Tonight!" Jesse hoped up from the bench. "At the party."

Caleb jerked away from Angie. "At the hotel's New Year's party?"

"Yes." Angie tried to compose herself. "What's wrong?"

"Jesse and I weren't planning to attend the party."

Angie's heart crashed against her chest. The disappointment pierced her. "I didn't know. I assumed you and Jesse would be at the party too. I'm sorry. I should have checked…"

"Please, Dad, we have to be at the party," Jesse said. "I have a surprise."

***

"Why don't we talk about this later?" Caleb stamped his left foot. He hoped to bring feeling back into his toes. As a child, he experienced frostbite after sledding for too long and still struggled with circulation in cold weather. A blustery wind blew snow across his cheeks. He took off his red plaid scarf and wove it around Jesse's neck. "It's really getting cold and I want to get you inside."

"Okay." Jesse pulled the scarf around his mouth. His shoulders slumped as he dragged his feet in the snow and headed up the hill toward the brightly lit Elmheart Hotel.

Caleb zipped his jacket with a hard yank. It wasn't easy being a single parent. Caleb hadn't been a very good dad for most of Jesse's young life. He'd missed so many of Jesse's milestones—his first word, first day of kindergarten and first time he brought home a positive report card. For years, Caleb placed drinking before Jesse. It was only after the car accident when Caleb sobered up. He'd been sober for almost a year.

"I'm sorry." Angie touched Caleb's arm. "I really didn't know you weren't attending the party. I taught Jesse to play a song. He wanted to perform for the guests. Hailey and Patrick said it would be okay."

"Thank you." Caleb looked down into Angie's blue eyes. His gaze trailed downward to her lips. What would it feel like to warm those lips with his? Caleb shook himself. What was he thinking? He was a former drunk who had a failed marriage under his belt and a seven-year-old son to raise. He was not the man for her. The past two weeks at the Elmheart Hotel, Caleb enjoyed listening to Angie's music. It reminded him of the summer when they worked in the amusement park theater. He loved nothing more than spending long nights with Angie. It was hard to be at home after his dad died. He and his mom never had anything to say to each other. Angie was softness, kindness and compassion. She always had a listening ear for him. When she left for the west coast, he felt as if there was a hole in his life. A hole he quickly filled with drinking and parties. Caleb cleared his throat. "How much do I owe you for the lessons?"

Angie stepped back. Her boots crunched in the snow as her eyes widened. "It's a gift." Angie lowered her voice. "Jesse took to the music very quickly. I enjoyed teaching him."

"Thanks." Caleb's words caught in his throat. Something inside him turned over. Angie found something in Jesse he struggled to see. Jesse didn't make friends at school. His teachers recommended he get involved in some activities. Caleb enrolled Jesse in the community after-school club. He hoped Jesse might enjoy some of the sports activities and find teammates to friend, but, Jesse wasn't interested in sports. At night, when Caleb attended his AA meetings, Jesse stayed at his grandma's house. Caleb's mom was an artist. She gave Jesse lessons in art—something he really enjoyed. Now, Caleb felt terrible. How had he overlooked Jesse's talents?

"He's a wonderful boy." Angie walked beside Caleb. Occasionally her feet slipped in the snow and she reached out her arms to steady herself. Ahead of them, Caitlin and Jesse chased each other and hurled snowballs.

Caleb pulled his jacket hood up over his knit cap. "I'm trying to give him a good holiday season. He misses his mom a lot, but he won't talk about it."

"Does he see her a lot?"

"No." Caleb's jaw clenched. His ex-wife, Wendy, decided Caleb wasn't any fun after he became sober. Wendy moved to New York City with a friend who promised parties every night. Wendy swore Jesse could visit as soon as she settled in her new apartment. There had been no invitation to visit. Instead, there was only an occasional phone call. It most often occurred when Wendy drank. Caleb intercepted the calls and they never reached Jesse.

"What did you have planned for New Year's Eve?" Angie asked.

"I hoped to have a quiet New Year's Eve. Jesse likes to play board games and pop popcorn."

"There isn't a special someone you'll kiss?" Angie glanced at him shyly.

"Nah." Caleb flushed. He was grateful his scarf hid his cheeks. He hadn't dated since he became sober. It was better to keep his life busy with AA meetings, Jesse and work. Caleb didn't want to run the risk of having a relationship send him spiraling back to drinking. He listened to the other men in AA. Many talked of relapses over a relationship, and he didn't want that to happen to him. It was more important for him to be there for Jesse as a clean and sober dad than to risk getting involved and have things go sour.

"So you and Jesse will bang pots and pans at New Year?" Angie asked. "I used to love banging pots and pans. I haven't done that in years."

"Yes." Caleb shrugged. "I'm sure it doesn't sound like a very exciting New Year's Eve to you."

"It sounds wonderful," Angie said. A wishful note crept into her voice.

Caleb glanced down at Angie. He assumed she was happy with her life. Since the day the hotel opened, Angie's music played in the hotel's speakers on a CD. Patrick raved about her to anyone who listened. Caleb couldn't help but notice Angie wore a gorgeous leather coat and matching leather boots. She talked about her expensive townhouse overlooking the Willamette River. Caleb didn't know what could be missing. But he heard the longing in her voice and wanted to do something for her.

"I hope Jesse enjoys the night," Caleb said, trying to explain his decision to both Angie and himself. "I want to make up for things in the past. When his mom and I were drinking, the party was at our house. I want to show him New Year's Eve without all the drunk partying."

"I understand," Angie said quietly. "Dad was always gone on New Year's Eve. It was one of the busiest nights at the bar." She pushed at the wrought iron gate of the hotel. A chunk of snow tumbled to her feet. The gate didn't budge.

"I've got it." Caleb stepped around Angie. He shoved the gate hard against the snow. "I need to shovel before someone hurts themselves."

Angie walked through the gate, but a large chunk of snow caught in the heel of her boot. She slipped and crashed against him.

"I got you." Caleb reached out to steady her. He wrapped his arms around her. For a minute, the world stopped. The snow fell around them. The lights from the hotel windows glowed. The holiday lights draped around the porch sparkled. Everything was perfect for just this one moment.

"Are you kissing?" Caitlin stood at the front door. She placed her hands on her hips. "It's not midnight yet."

Angie quickly pulled away from Caleb. She giggled nervously and headed for the open door. Caleb followed behind. He felt as if they had just been caught at the doorstep by a parent after a date. Caleb tried to control the pounding of his heart. Don't get carried away, he warned himself. Angie was only in his arms because of the snow and ice—nothing more. Even it was something more, there would be no use getting attached. Keep it even and steady.

In the front hallway, Caleb shrugged out of his coat and untied his scarf. Guests gathered in the living room on couches and chairs. Some read while others played board games. A blazing fire roared in the fireplace and a silver tray filled with hot chocolate and marshmallows sat on the dining room table. The Christmas tree sparkled. A few decorative boxes lay underneath on a gold and red tree skirt. Jesse sat at the dining room table and drank a cup of cocoa. Caleb couldn't wait to grab a cup of hot chocolate and warm up. He would talk to Jesse about New Year's Eve. Maybe there was a way to allow Jesse to play his song on New Year's Day before the guests checked out. Snow fell outside the large picture window in the living room. Caleb made a mental note to hurry with his snack. He and Jesse needed to head home before the storm got any worse. They didn't live too far from the hotel, but far enough that a walk in the cold snow would not be good for Jesse.

194

Mrs. Anderson tapped his left arm. "The lamp in my room doesn't work." Her dark eyes stared at Caleb. Grey curly hair framed her narrow face. She was already dressed in a black evening dress, even though the New Year party didn't start for another couple hours.

"It doesn't?" Caleb frowned. When Mrs. Anderson checked into the hotel, she insisted the light wasn't working. Caleb looked and everything seemed to be in order. But, Mrs. Anderson demanded he take apart the lamp. While he worked, she settled into a plush armchair beside the bed. Caleb quickly learned this was the first holiday after her husband's death. She and her sister shared one of the second floor double bed rooms. Hailey hadn't wanted to put two beds in a room. She said it made the room too small. But hotel decorator Jenny, insisted. There would be guests traveling together who wanted to share a room, but not a bed. Hailey relented and the room was one of the first booked for the holidays.

"No." Mrs. Anderson repeated. "It doesn't work."

"Mmm....I'll have to take a look," Caleb said. The last two times Mrs. Anderson insisted the light didn't work, Caleb replaced the bulb. He didn't know what he would do this time. Caleb looked around the room for Jesse. He wanted to take him upstairs so they could leave quickly afterwards. But instead of Jesse, Caleb locked eyes with Angie. She smiled at him. Caleb stuffed his hands into his pockets. He leaned back on his heels and returned the smile.

"Caleb? Angie?" Patrick stepped out of the kitchen. He wore a white apron and his dark hair looked frizzy. "Can you come with me a minute?" He motioned toward the small room off the back of the living room. The room had been an old porch which Hailey and Patrick converted into the hotel office.

Caleb turned to Mrs. Anderson. "I'll be right up to check it out."

"Thank you." She clasped his hands. "You're a good man. I hope you find a special new love in the New Year."

Caleb felt his ears burn. He didn't dare look at Angie and hurried into the small office.

A large oak desk sat in the middle of the room. Three sets of bookshelves lined the walls. Hailey sat at the desk. She typed furiously on the computer. Manila folders were stacked in a red and green basket by her side. Each folder was labeled with a breakfast recipe. Hailey looked up with a tense smile. She'd pulled her hair up into a ponytail and without make-up, she looked more like a college student than the owner of the hotel. "Good news. Bad news," she said.

Patrick shut the heavy oak door. "I'm sorry to do this on New Year's Eve, but I need a little help. Our good friend, Sadie, is having her twins."

"That's the good news." Hailey chimed in.

"What's the bad news?" Caleb shifted on his feet. Angie stood directly in front of him. Her shoulders stiffened.

"Sadie and Damon own a bed and breakfast in Rochester," Patrick continued. "She asked if Hailey can come over to help with the guests until Damon's parents can get here from Syracuse. They have a full house."

"A New Year's baby." Angie's voice lifted in excitement. "Maybe it will be the first baby born in the New Year."

"What can we do to help?" Caleb asked. Patrick had given him a job when no one else wanted to hire him. People didn't trust him. No one would hire him until he proved he could stay sober. But Patrick took a chance on him. He would do anything to pay him back.

"I'm going to drive Hailey to the bed and breakfast. But, we may not make it back for the New Year party. I know this is a lot to ask but—"

"We can take care of things," Caleb said.

"Yes," Angie said firmly. "We can handle the hotel party."

"Jesse will be very happy to find out his surprise will happen after all," Caleb said, and chuckled.

"Yes he will," Angie said, and turned to face Caleb.

Caleb stepped closer to Angie. He placed his hands on her shoulders and squeezed. "It will be just like working at the theater, right?"

"Right," Angie said slowly. Her voice sounded unsteady and hesitant.

Caleb searched Angie's face. Was Angie happy about the new plans?

***

Gold streamers dangled from the ballroom ceiling. Silver and gold New Year balloons hung from each table chair. In the far corner of the room, Caleb polished a stubborn spot on the wood trim. His sweatshirt lay on the floor and his muscles moved beneath his long-sleeved shirt. Angie tried hard not to stare as she inserted gold ribbon through table place cards. Jesse and Caitlin sat at the piano bench and practiced Jesse's song. Every once in a while, Caitlin's voice rose above the notes Jesse played as she barked out instructions. Angie smiled. Caitlin didn't know any more about playing the piano than Jesse, but she excelled at telling others what to do. Angie tied another gold ribbon to a white place card. She set it in a stack to the left of her at the large rectangular table. Ellen Matthews, Hailey's grandmother and the first owner of the Elmheart Hotel, attached a silver ribbon to small bags of confetti. Short grey hair framed her heart-shaped face. "What are you wearing to the party, dear?"

"I brought a pair of black slacks and a white blouse." Angie lowered her eyes and bit her lip. "It's not very fancy. I hoped to be able to do some shopping, but the time got away from me." At the last minute, Angie decided not to bring her long black evening dress. It seemed too formal for the small inn's party. Hailey told her there was a new boutique shop in town and they could do some New Year shopping. But, the holidays slipped by so fast and, now with the snowstorm, shopping was out of the picture. Angie stole another peak at Caleb as he moved the rag back and forth. He worked his way closer to her and his muscles flexed with each movement. What would it be like to run her hands over those muscles? What it would it feel like to have his lips on hers? Caleb looked up and his eyes met hers. She flushed and quickly turned away.

She hoped he couldn't see the desire and longing on her face.

"I know just the place to find something to wear." Ellen placed the last bag of confetti in a wicker basket. "There are some old trunks in the attic. A long time ago, I sewed for the theater. When it closed, the costume trunks were stored here. Everyone hoped the theater would open again."

"It's a great theater." Caleb stepped up beside the table. "I'd really love to see it brought back to life. This town needs some of the arts."

Angie turned and looked up at Caleb. She softened her voice and leaned toward him. "You should do it."

Caleb's eyes warmed as he gazed down at her. "Maybe." He lowered his right hand to her shoulder and squeezed. "Thanks for the encouragement."

Angie shivered under his touch and her belly warmed.

"And what are you wearing to the party?" Ellen asked brightly.

Caleb's ears turned pink. He removed his hand from Angie's shoulder. "I don't have anything fancier than my old jeans and sweatshirt."

"That settles it." Ellen rose from her chair. "Meet me on the third floor at the end of the hall."

"By the attic stairs?" Caleb raised his right eyebrow.

"Shhh…" Ellen placed her finger to her lips. "Those stairs are supposed to be a secret."

"I'm the handyman," Caleb said and chuckled. "I know all the secrets."

Suddenly, Jesse banged his hands on the keys of the piano. Caitlin's voice rose in a shrill command.

Caleb quickly turned toward the piano as though he planned to referee the two.

"I will check on Jesse and Caitlin." Angie stood, and pushed in her chair. She placed her hand lightly on Caleb's arm before she headed to the piano. She needed a few minutes to regain her composure. All afternoon, she'd felt out of control. Her heart raced every time Caleb looked at her. Her stomach fluttered and her chest filled with a longing and desire. But, she was leaving in another day and a half. She didn't want to start something which could only end in heartache for both of them.

Angie strode to the piano. "What is wrong?"

"Jesse won't listen to me," Caitlin said. "The song doesn't sound right."

"I played the right note." Jesse pushed Caitlin to the far left side of the piano bench. "I played it the way you taught me."

"Play it for me." Angie leaned against the side of the piano. Next to her, Caleb grabbed his sweatshirt and pulled it on. Angie tried hard not to watch every movement. She redirected her attention back to listening to Jesse play the piano.

The disconnected notes rang in her ears. "Mmmm…." Caitlin was right. Jesse didn't play the right notes. "Let me see if I can show you."

Angie sat down at the piano and quickly played the correct notes.

"That's what I played," Jesse insisted.

"Why don't you let me play the song for a few minutes?" Angie suggested.

A dark shadow crossed Jesse's face. He placed his hands over his chest and balled his fists. "I quit."

"No," Angie said quickly. "I didn't mean it like that. When I get confused or frustrated, it helps to listen to someone else play. It's like inspiration for my playing."

Jesse's lower lip trembled.

"Listen." She ran her fingers over the notes in a couple quick scales. Then without thinking, Angie played the song she performed every summer. The notes rushed back to her and she allowed herself to get lost in the music. The memories of Caleb and the cool summer evenings flashed through her mind.

When she finished, the sound of clapping filled the ballroom. Angie looked up and across the room to Caleb. He stood in the doorway and stared at her with a hunger in his eyes that took her breath away.

"Your cheeks are red," Caitlin said.

"Playing the piano is hard work," Angie mumbled. She couldn't break her gaze with Caleb. His eyes mirrored her emotions.

"Can I have some hot chocolate?" Jesse asked, and touched her sleeve. "I think hot chocolate will make me play better."

"Of course." Angie cleared her throat. She shifted on the piano bench and broke her gaze with Caleb.

Caitlin and Jesse flew from the room, as though all arguments were forgotten. Slowly, Angie wound her way to the entryway and Caleb. When she reached the doorway, she looked up into Caleb's eyes. He placed a hand on her shoulder and stared at her. "I have never forgotten that song. Will you play it tonight?" His fingers crept into her hair and softly, he stroked the back of her neck.

"I don't know," Angie whispered. She couldn't find her voice. "I'm not sure it's in my set tonight."

Caleb's fingers played their own song on her neck. "I'd like to hear it again," he said softly. He twirled a piece of her hair in his fingers.

Angie's heart melted. She knew it was wrong. She couldn't promise Caleb anything—but she wanted him. She wanted him to kiss her, to hold her in his arms and never let go.

"Dad!" Jesse hollered from the hallway. "Mrs. Matthews is looking for you and Angie."

"I guess we should go." Caleb's eyes darkened as he gazed at her.

"Yes," Angie said weakly.

Her legs felt rubbery as she followed Caleb into the living room. A large fire burned in the fireplace. Four of the guests played a game of Scrabble. The mayor raised his hand and waved. "We're looking forward to the party tonight and hearing you play."

"Thank you." Angie nodded toward them. A CD of her music played on the stereo. She performed the song often in concerts and recitals. But something didn't sound right. The song played technically correct but it lacked something. Angie frowned. Maybe the reviews were right— her music lacked something.

"Coming?" Caleb turned to her from the stairs.

"Yes." Angie pushed away her thoughts. A red ribbon lay on the stair landing. Angie leaned over and picked it up. She retied the ribbon and walked briskly down the hallway to where a pull-down ladder stretched to the plush carpet. A light shone from the attic above. Cold air raced down her spine. She wrapped her arms around herself. The thin black sweater she wore didn't keep the chill out of her body.

"Wear this." Caleb yanked his sweatshirt over his head and held it out to her.

"Thank you." Angie took the piece of clothing from Caleb's outstretched hands. She pulled the warm sweatshirt over her. It was like being wrapped in Caleb's arms. His woodsy pine scent drifted around her. She snuggled deeper into the warmth.

"After you." Caleb waved to the stairs.

Angie grabbed onto the railing and hoisted herself up to the attic. A single bulb lit the attic space. Trunks and boxes covered almost every spare inch.

"I really need to get up here and clean this out." Ellen stood in the middle of the room. She placed her hands on her hips "But I just haven't the heart. There is so much history stored in these boxes. I thought maybe Hailey would like to go through it one day."

Angie turned around slowly. Boxes of all sizes were stacked in the far right hand corner with each holiday labeled neatly on them. Rows of trunks lined the east side and a set of suitcases were stacked neatly on the west side.

"The costumes are over here somewhere." Ellen whirled in a small circle. She peered into the dark corners as more snow covered the vents in the attic roof.

"I have a flashlight up here." Caleb strode to a large box at the edge of the attic pulled out a large yellow flashlight and shone the light at the edges of the attic.

Angie ran her hand over the rough top of a brown trunk. "These trunks look really old. "They look as though they could have been stagecoach trunks."

"That's the one." Ellen's voice rose in excitement.

Angie undid the silver latch. She slowly pulled up the lid. The smell of mothballs engulfed her. Angie reached into the trunk and grabbed a handful of shiny black fabric. She shook out a 1920's evening gown. The waist dropped low below the neckline. Silver beads covered the dress. "I love it!" Angie exclaimed. She held it up to her-self "Do you think it fits me?"

"I think it will be perfect," Ellen said. "And if not, I have my sewing machine downstairs. We can always adjust it."

"I found some shoes over here," Caleb called.

Angie hurried to a second trunk pushed against the window. Her heart lifted at each new find. She hadn't enjoyed dressing up this much since she played dress-up as a child with her mom's clothing. She peered inside the trunk. Rows of shoes lined the trunk on small shelves. Angie pulled out a pair of black and white men's dress shoes. She held them up to Caleb. "What are you wearing tonight? I think these would be perfect."

"Whooah." Caleb whistled. "Those are some shoes." He took one from Angie and held it up to the light. "There is a tuxedo in here that will fit me just fine and a bow tie to go with it." Caleb turned over a black and white tie in his hand. "It matches the shoes."

"I think I saw a smaller bow tie," Angie said. "It's something for Jesse to wear too."

"I'm so glad everything is working out." Ellen headed for the stairs. "I'll check on the guests. If you need anything, please call for me."

"I think we're almost done." Angie clutched the dress tightly to her chest. "We'll make sure the trunks are shut tight."

Angie turned back to the trunk. A thin, lacy pale peach slip hung out of the side. She carefully pulled it out and held it up to her face.

"Mmmm...." Caleb's voice sounded husky and deep.

Angie gazed upward into Caleb's hungry eyes. She couldn't look away and her hands shook. He took a step closer to her. Her heart pounded but she didn't move.

"Angie." Caleb's eyes trailed down to her lips.

"Caleb," Angie whispered.

His arms wrapped around her and the slip fluttered to the ground. She wound her hands through his hair. A passion inside her ignited as she raised her face and closed her eyes. A deep sigh escaped her as Caleb's lips met hers.

***

Caleb pulled Angie closer to him and deepened the kiss. He trailed his fingers in a soft caress along the side of her face. She sighed and moved closer to him.

"Dad?" Jesse shouted. "Angie?"

"Mmmm...." Reluctantly, Caleb pulled away from Angie. He looked down at her. She gazed shyly up at him as he picked up her hand and intertwined their fingers. "We'll finish this later," he said softly.

Jesse's round face appeared at the attic stairs. "What are you doing?" He hopped into the attic and, without looking at Caleb and Angie, headed for the open trunk. "Look at this great hat!" He pulled out a large black top hat and placed it on his head. Jesse tapped his feet and whirled in circles. "Do you think there are tap shoes? I am a great dancer."

"I think piano playing is enough for tonight," Caleb said. "But there is something you can wear in these trunks. We found a suit coat for you and a bow tie."

"Great!" Jesse stopped dancing and rubbed his stomach. "Is it time to eat?"

"It's past time to eat." Angie cleared her throat and checked her gold watch. "It's almost time to begin the concert. We've got to get changed. The guests will wonder if there is going to be a New Year's party."

Angie picked up the pale peach slip and the dress. She hurried to the attic stairs. Caleb motioned for Jesse to follow her. He grabbed the bow ties and suit jackets for himself and Jesse, then turned off the light and clamored down behind Jesse. By the time Caleb reached the third floor landing, Angie had already stepped into her bedroom at the end of the hall. She flashed him a smile. "See you for the show." She still wore his sweatshirt.

"Is Angie going to be my new mom?" Jesse took Caleb's hand and yanked him toward the staircase.

Caleb shifted the shoes and bow tie from his right to left hand. He placed a hand on Jesse's left shoulder. "Why do you ask that?"

"You kissed her and I saw you hold her hand. Andrew's parents kiss and hold hands. I never saw you kiss Mom and hold her hand." Jesse's voice lowered. "I like Angie. If she was my mom, I would learn lots of new songs."

Caleb's stomach tied into knots and he rubbed his eyes. Reality crashed into him. Why didn't he think before he kissed Angie? In the last two weeks, Jesse had become very attached to Angie. He couldn't mislead him into thinking he and Angie would be together. It wasn't possible. Caleb kneeled beside Jesse and stared him square in the eye. "I like Angie, too. And you did see Angie and me kiss. But Angie has a very busy life. She lives far away..." Caleb broke off. The words stuck in his throat.

"We could move," Jesse said cheerfully.

Jesse's eyes sparkled. His face lit with hope. He so badly wanted a family. But, how could Caleb give that to him with Angie? Angie deserved to be with a man who could accompany her to recitals and enjoy long romantic dinners. She did not need a man who had a seven-year-old son and whose life revolved around AA meetings. "Angie is a very special person," Caleb said, "but we have a life here. Angie has a life on the west coast." He could not give Jesse what he wanted. He couldn't give himself what he wanted, either.

"Are you going to kiss Angie at midnight?" Jesse asked. "I would kiss Angie at midnight." Jesse yanked his top hat down and over his eyes. He grinned at Caleb.

Caleb squeezed Jesse's shoulders. "I'll remember that. Now go get dressed for the party." Caleb handed Jesse the small suit coat from the attic. He took a deep breath. He had a job to do. He promised Patrick. He needed to set aside his romantic thoughts of Angie and focus on his job. In another day and a half, Angie would be gone and everything would go back to normal. He just needed to get through the party and snowstorm.

By the time Caleb dressed and returned downstairs, guests mingled in the ballroom where Ellen Matthews strolled through with silver trays of appetizers. Caitlin worked in the kitchen and helped to refill the appetizer trays with small sandwiches. Angie's light music filled the room. Candles glowed on the long dining room table and thick snow fell outside the window. The scent of pine drifted through the room from the tall tree that stood in the corner.

"Can I play my song now?" Jesse tugged on Caleb's black dress coat.

"Why don't we check with Angie?" Caleb walked with Jesse over to the piano. He couldn't stop staring at Angie. In the candlelight, her eyes glimmered and her skin shone.

Caleb cleared his throat. He felt like a twelve-year old boy asking a girl to dance. "Jesse wants to play his song. Is this a good time?"

"Why don't you let me play a few more songs and encourage people to dance? Then, we'll have your song." Angie smiled at Jesse. Warmth filled her eyes.

"Okay." Jesse stood straight as a board next to the piano. "My stomach feels funny. I think I'm a little bit nervous."

"It's okay, bud." Caleb pulled Jesse close to him. "Why don't you help me entertain the guests with a few old time stories?"

Angie smiled at him, and without missing a note, moved into a show tune with a lively tempo. Caitlin whisked by and grabbed Jesse's hand. "It's time to dance." Her pink party dress twirled to her knees and black patent leather shoes tapped on the shiny floor. A handful of couples laughed and followed them onto the dance floor.

"Great job." Caleb winked at Angie. "I'll go work my theater magic."

For the next few hours, Angie played song after song. Guests flowed from the ballroom, to the table and into the living room. Caleb moved among them, telling funny stories about the Elmheart hotel, the town and the lively people who built the town. When Jesse and Cailtin became tired of dancing, they pulled out board games in the living room and a few of the guests joined them.

At eleven-thirty, Caleb motioned for Jesse it was time to play his song.

Jesse's face paled and he bit his lower lip. Slowly, he walked into the ballroom and to the piano. When Jesse reached the piano, Angie leaned close to him. "I'll sit with you. It can be scary the first time you play a song for others."

Jesse sat beside Angie on the bench. He placed his hands on the keys. A simple melody filled the room. The guests turned toward him and the room went silent as Jesse's simple tune quickly turned into a joyful expression of a young boy performing for the first time. From across the ballroom, Caleb's chest expanded with pride. As Jesse played, Caleb stole a quick look at Angie. Her sequin gown sparkled and a gold necklace with matching earrings hung from her ears. She lit up the room. Caleb's heart filled with emotions. He was in love with her. He had been since the time they worked together at the amusement park, but they lived two very different lives. The best thing he could do would be to think of this night as only a holiday memory and let her go. Caleb balled his hands into a fist and stuck them in his pocket. He eyed the bar longingly. Just one drink would make all his intense feelings about falling in love with Angie disappear.

"He's a good boy." Mrs. Anderson tapped his arm. "He plays very well."

"Yes," Caleb said. The desire to drink faded away as he remembered his purpose—to be a good dad. "He is a wonderful boy." He smiled at Mrs. Anderson, grateful to her for reminding him of his role.

At the end of the song, the guests broke into applause. Jesse jumped off the piano bench and bowed. Angie slipped into Jesse's place and a familiar song filled the ballroom. Caleb closed his eyes and leaned back against the wall. He remembered a bright-eyed eighteen-year-old girl who enchanted him with her music and her warm compassion. It was a summer when he believed anything was possible because Angie believed in him. When the song ended, Caleb opened his eyes and found Angie watching him.

***

Angie stepped into the warm kitchen and shut the door behind her. She leaned against the door. Her heart pounded. For the last two hours, she had done nothing but focus on her performance. She pushed all thoughts of Caleb's kiss and how it felt to be in his arms, out of her mind. She felt grateful for her smooth playing and ability to keep her mind on her job. It wasn't until Jesse performed that Angie felt her heart go to pieces. Caleb was so proud of Jesse and she felt like a tornado struck inside her. She loved teaching Jesse music. She loved spending family time at the hotel with her niece and brother and sister-in-law. But, most important, she loved to spend time with Caleb.

"Angie?" Ellen sat at the round kitchen table. She placed party noisemakers next to each champagne glass on the silver tray. Her nimble fingers moved quickly until the tray was full and the bag empty. "Are you okay?"

Angie jumped. "Yes." She shook her head. "No." Angie clutched her black wrap close. "I'm not returning to the west coast." The words spilled out of her.

"Are you sure?" Ellen asked. "You have built a very successful career. There is nothing here like what you have out west."

"Things have not been going well. I'm not happy," Angie confessed. "But, this holiday season, I've been so happy. I've loved spending time with Caitlin. I've enjoyed getting to know Hailey better and reconnecting with Patrick. Jesse is wonderful."

"And?"

"Caleb," Angie said quietly. "I love spending time with Caleb."

"There are no concert halls here," Ellen said. "No large performance recitals. What will you do?"

"I've been thinking about things," Angie said. Her tone lightened as the ideas she played over in her mind during the last few days took shape. "I like teaching Jesse music. I'd like to spend some more time teaching kids and adults to play. There is also that theater. Maybe someday, there would be need of a concert pianist." Angie's heart lifted as the images filled her mind. She could have a life here. It wouldn't be as grand as the one she enjoyed in Portland, but it would be a life rich with family and friends. The grandfather clock struck eleven-forty-five in the dining room.

"It's almost midnight ." Ellen's eyes sparkled as she picked up a tray of champagne glasses. "Shall we toast the New Year?"

Angie smiled and lifted up one of the trays. She had a new life to toast. She turned to find Caleb leaning against the doorway. A small smile played around his lips. "You're staying?"

"Yes," Angie's voice shook, but she did not waiver. "I am staying."

Caleb stepped forward and hoisted the tray from her hands. "Let me carry that." Caleb's fingers touched hers and lightly caressed her hand.

Suddenly, Caitlin burst from the ballroom. She held the hotel phone in her left hand and jumped up and down. Her pink dress sash floated to the ground and she danced in stocking feet, her shoes left behind on the ballroom floor. "Sadie had her twins. Dad just called. He said everyone is doing great. He wished us a Happy New Year."

As if on cue, the grandfather clock struck twelve.

"I've got to get to the piano," Angie said, her brow furrowed into a frown. "It's midnight. Everyone is expecting Auld Lang Syne."

"You're not leaving without a New Year kiss." Caleb set the tray down. He wrapped his arms around her and lowered his lips to hers. "Happy New Year, Angie."

"Happy New Year, Caleb." Angie melted into his warm embrace.

Happy New Year!

Dear Reader,

The story's setting for Vintage Valentine, Halloween Love Fortune and New Year Heart Song is the Elmheart Hotel. The Elmheart was a hotel on the shores of Lake Ontario during the late 1800's. The hotel was the last stop on a trolley line that ran from Rochester, New York to Manitou Beach. Fredrick Odenbach built the hotel in the early 1890's. However, the Skinner family, who owned the land next to the hotel, claimed the hotel was on their land. They took Odenbach to court. The court ruled the land belonged to Odenbach.

The Skinner family still thought the hotel belonged to them, and they took Odenbach to court again. This time, the ruling was in favor of the Skinner family. The mix-up in ownership happened over a surveyor mistake in 1802. The property line was declared at an oak tree. But, the tree was really an elm tree. After the court ruled in favor of Skinner, he gave the hotel the name The Elmheart Hotel.

In 1903, the hotel was sold to Michael Olaughlin and George Weidman. A room fire in 1931 forced George to stop renting rooms to guests. However, during the Depression, George built a dance hall next to the hotel. Big bands played in the dance hall and the hotel was kept open only as a bar on evenings and weekends. After George's death in 1986, there was talk of building a restaurant and restoring the hotel. But, due to a lack of sewer systems, the plans never moved forward.

In 1990, a boyfriend took me to see the hotel. The windows were boarded up, the paint peeling and the yard was filled with weeds. However, the old ballroom was still intact. I fell in love with the Elmheart Hotel and envisioned how it could be restored. The hotel burned in 1993 and arson was listed as the cause of the fire. My dream never materialized, but I hope this series of sweet, contemporary novellas restores the Elmheart Hotel and gives it a happily-ever-after.

If you enjoyed, New Year Heart Song, be sure to read the first Elmheart Hotel story about Hailey, Patrick and Caitlin in Vintage Valentine and Jenny and Zach's story in the second story in the series, Halloween Love Fortune. And, to read more about Sadie and Damon's love story, check out Love's Storms, the first novella in my sweet, contemporary Sailor Series published by Books To Go Now.

Happy New Year!
Mindy Hardwick

ABOUT THE AUTHOR
MINDY HARDWICK

Mindy Hardwick enjoys writing for teens and tweens, and, sometimes, you can catch her writing contemporary, sweet romances. STAINED GLASS SUMMER is a middle grade coming-of-age novel and an EPIC Ebook Award Finalist in Children's, and WEAVING MAGIC is a young adult romance. Mindy's contemporary, sweet romance stories include: VINTAGE VALENTINE, LOVE'S STORMS, LOVE'S BID, and LOVE'S CHRISTMAS GIFT. Mindy runs a poetry workshop with teens in a juvenile detention. She says that her best ideas come from the teens. To find out about Mindy's latest writing adventures, please sign up for Mindy Hardwick's blog or visit Mindy Hardwick's website.

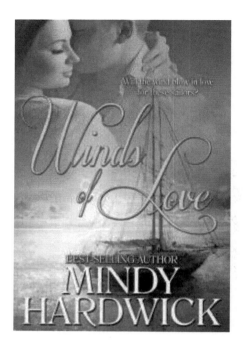

Winds of Love Anthology

Winds of Love, a short story anthology from best-selling author, Mindy Hardwick. Three, short, sweet contemporary romances together for the first time. Will the wind blow in love for these sailors?

Love's Storm: Surrendering to love is not easy, will it take a storm to show Sabrina and Damon that some things are worth holding onto?

Love's Bid: Cassie Richardson enjoys serving as President of the Sailing Club Foundation Board and overseeing the smooth running of operations. But, when former boyfriend, Eric Atkins, steps in to fill the role of Board Treasurer, things begin spiraling out of control. Will a bidding war be enough to overcome the past?

Love's Christmas Gift: Skipper Bill and Elizabeth have been friends forever. But, when Elizabeth is offered a job interview across the country, these two friends are going to need the help of a little mistletoe to find their holiday romance.

10746513R00129

Made in the USA
San Bernardino, CA
25 April 2014